MW00509467

NEKROMANCER'S CAGE

KATHRYN ROSSATI

Copyright (C) 2020 Kathryn Rossati

Layout design and Copyright (C) 2020 by Next Chapter

Published 2021 by Next Chapter

Edited by Tyler Colins

Cover art by Cover Mint

Back cover texture by David M. Schrader, used under license from Shutterstock.com

Mass Market Paperback Edition

This book is a work of fiction. Names, characters, places, and incidents are the product of the author's imagination or are used fictitiously. Any resemblance to actual events, locales, or persons, living or dead, is purely coincidental.

All rights reserved. No part of this book may be reproduced or transmitted in any form or by any means, electronic or mechanical, including photocopying, recording, or by any information storage and retrieval system, without the author's permission.

CHAPTER 1

'*H*ere, let me,' Johnathan said, easily loosening the knot on his mentor's apron strings so they fell free, enabling the old man to lift it off over his head with shaking hands. It pained Johnathan to see how much Alfred had deteriorated already.

Johnathan had studied under Alfred for three years, learning all there was to know about remedial Alkemy, from how to define a customer's problems to mixing the right powders for their medicine. The work had been hard, but under his mentor's guidance, Johnathan had slowly picked it up until he was proficient; in another year, he would have been able to take his exam and become an Alkemical Apothecary himself. Yet, for the time being at least, that dream would have to be put on hold.

Alfred had been diagnosed with Acute Energy Loss, a disease which had no cure and soon would leave him bedridden, unable to work at all. And because Johnathan was not yet qualified to take over, the Board of Alkemists had deemed it necessary to close the shop for good. Alfred's clients had taken their business elsewhere, and all that was left to do now was to finish packing up their well-used equipment.

'Thank you, my boy. We've only got one job left,' Alfred said softly, resting on a stool next to the carefully packed boxes containing the many tools and ingredients he'd used daily for the past forty years. 'The lettering outside needs to be scraped off.'

Johnathan cast his eyes to the floor, a cold, empty feeling settling in his stomach. Scraping away the sign had such a finality to it. He wasn't sure if he was ready. 'But I'll need a ladder for that. Do we even have one?' he asked, knowing full well that there was one tucked away in the back cupboard, half rotten and full of cobwebs.

'A ladder?' Alfred chuckled warmly. 'Nonsense, John. You're a gangly young thing; hop up on one of those stools and I'm sure you'll be able to reach it. There's a metal scraper in the second drawer to your right. I left it out especially. It should be sharp enough to do the job.'

Opening the drawer, Johnathan found the scraper, a short-handled tool with a flat, triangular blade. He tested it with his thumb and concluded that it was indeed sharp enough. After sprinkling a mix of powders over his newly-earnt cut to help stop the bleeding, he reluctantly gathered one of the round wooden stools and headed outside to where the words 'A. Vancold: Alkemical Apothecary' were stencilled above the shop's broad windows in large, white lettering.

Despite being tall, one of Johnathan's biggest fears was heights. Even being a few feet off the ground as he was then, trying to balance himself on the stool's small seat, was enough to make him dizzy.

Still, he couldn't leave this job to Alfred. If the old man exerted himself too much, it would only advance his condition, and by order of the Board of Alkemists, the shop had to be completely bare by the time they were due to leave the premises that afternoon.

So, gripping the outer wall for dear life, Johnathan steeled himself and began scraping the words away. The peelings floated down to the floor like snowflakes, and by the time he was finished, real snow was beginning to fall from the darkening sky.

'Well, John,' Alfred said when Johnathan finally came back inside. 'I think that's everything.'

With their hearts heavy, they loaded all the boxes of equipment and ingredients into the motor carriage that the Board of Alkemists had provided and then locked the front door before giving the keys to the driver. The driver put them in a small, secure black case and then ticked off the equipment on a list attached to a smart clipboard. Satisfied everything was there, he gave Alfred a single Ren coin for each box and then got into the motor carriage and drove off, taking their whole livelihood with him to be stored in the Board's warehouse. All except for one small, neatly stitched travel bag.

With his mouth twitched up in a crooked grin, Alfred held the bag out to Johnathan. 'I can't do much to help you continue your studies, but at least I managed to save you these. It's only a small selection, mind, but it should be enough to deal with some common ailments, at least.'

Johnathan took it and peered inside; dozens of tightly packed packets filled it to the brim, each neatly labelled in Alfred's handwriting. A bundle of ingredients like that was worth more than two week's pay! 'I

... can't accept this, Alfred,' he said, trying to hold back the emotion in his voice. 'You should keep them; after all, the shop was yours.'

Alfred shook his head. 'My time is over, John. I'm too old and certainly too tired to do any dispensing harder than making tea. Take them. I'm sure they'll come in handy.' He inhaled deeply and put his hands on Johnathan's shoulders. 'You'll make a fine Alkemical Apothecary one day, my boy, I'm sure of it. Don't let this stop you from achieving your goals. It will take a while to find another shop to finish your apprenticeship at, but you *will* find one. Anyone worth their salt will see just how good you are if you show them.'

With that, Alfred wrapped his thick cloak tightly about him as a chilling wind blew through the street, and with one last glance at the empty green shop, turned and walked away.

Johnathan stood for a moment, letting the snowflakes build up in his black hair so that, in the light of the alkemically charged Kerical lamps flickering on every few feet throughout the street, he looked just as grey as Alfred had.

He'd been fourteen when he began his apprenticeship at the shop, a teenager full of enthusiasm and energy, eager to learn every detail about remedial Alkemy there was, and also some of the general Alkemy that Alfred often spoke about.

His parents had been less than thrilled with his career choice; in a city as big as Nodnol, where nearly everything used Alkemy or Kerical energy – a modern fusion of Alkemy and Lectric energy – it was hard to make a name for oneself in the small, selective circle of Alkemy-based Apothecaries. But Johnathan had ignored their snide comments and attempts to make him interested in a different school of Alkemy (like engineering, which was an ever-expanding field far from short of opportunity), and as soon as he'd finished his final school year, he had run to Alfred and begged him to take him on as his apprentice.

At the time, Alfred hadn't been thrilled either. He'd had hundreds of customers daily and scant time to teach Johnathan even the basics. But the boy had stood and listened to every conversation, watched every tiny measure of powder or mix of dry ingredients until Alfred only had to say the slightest word and Johnathan would be dashing to the well-stocked drawers and jars to fetch everything his mentor needed. They made a good team, and as Johnathan's knowledge expanded, both from Alfred's guidance and from his textbooks on theory provided by the Board, he found alternative ways of grinding and mixing that improved the longevity and potency of the medicine without any changes to the ingredients.

Now that time was over, and Johnathan had to move on. Shaking the snow off his head, he reluctantly pulled the shutters over the shop windows for the last time, and like Alfred had done ten minutes before, turned to head home.

It was bitterly cold, and some of the lamps flickered in distaste as the wind rattled them from side to side. Holding the bag close and turning the collar of his long coat up to try and warm his ears, Johnathan trudged through the throng of people milling about, making his way across the square. Even this late in the evening, Nodnol's shops and factories were buzzing with activity. There were whole emporiums of spas and beauty parlours, florists, clockmakers, motor carriage garages, haberdasheries, tailors, food markets and a hundred others. Chimneys puffed out colours from across the spectrum, vibrant oranges and pinks to inky purples and blues, every one of them reflecting off the settling snow, and no matter where Johnathan looked, the hum of the city's determination and drive rattled through him. Normally, he found it inspiring, but today it was mocking, laughing at his and Alfred's misfortune. All he wanted to do was get away from it.

After twenty minutes, he finally turned the corner and saw the familiar apartment building where he was currently living. It was hardly luxurious, built from grey brick and set back slightly from the buildings on either side so that it was constantly cast in shadow, but the rooms were spacious enough for what Johnathan needed and, more importantly considering his apprentice's wage, cheap. Most of the other tenants were people who worked long hours and lived on their own, so it wasn't unusual for professionals to move in – they didn't care where they lived, as long as they could get their work done, even if they could afford somewhere more expensive. They were always nice enough if Johnathan happened to bump into them, but very rarely did they offer more than a few pleasantries.

He put his key in the lock of the main door and turned it, hearing it click. With a practiced nudge to encourage the rusted hinges into motion, the door opened, and he walked into the hall beyond, about to go upstairs to his rooms. Unfortunately, the noise of his entrance had aroused the attention of Mrs Higgins, the landlady, whose own apartment was just down the hall, and before he could even acknowledge her approach, she was standing in front of him.

'So, this was it, was it? Your last day at that shabby old shop?' she asked acidly, adjusting her stiff skirts. Despite being a foot shorter than Johnathan and in her late seventies, Mrs Higgins was one of those people who have such a commanding presence that it's impossible to ignore them. He sometimes thought it was the severity of her eyes, or perhaps the fact that her clothes were so rigid, they demanded extreme discipline simply to wear them.

'Uh, yes, Mrs Higgins. We closed the shop down today,' he replied. 'But don't worry, I've got enough money for two months' rent, at least.'

Her eyes narrowed. 'Are you certain? I don't want to hold on to that apartment for you with no income, when I know there are far more reliable people around to rent it.'

Johnathan swallowed. Her gaze was so penetrating that he couldn't help but feel like a child under it. 'Yes, ma'am, I'm certain. And I won't be hanging around just waiting for my money to run out. From tomorrow morning, I'll be looking for another Alkemical Apothecary to apprentice with, I promise you.'

'Very well, but if I get even a whiff of you being an idle layabout, I'll have you out of here faster than you can blink. Now, be gone with you, I'm tired. Oh, and if you catch Mr Edwards on your way up, tell him that *his* rent needs paying for this month. I haven't seen hide nor hair of him for days.'

'I'll let him know. Uh, goodnight, ma'am,' Johnathan said, and hurried up the stairs without giving her the chance to say anything else.

He dashed into his apartment and threw his things on the chair, and then rushed to the apartment opposite, where Mr Edwards lived. He knocked urgently on the door. There was no answer.

'Mr Edwards?' he called, knocking again. 'Mr Edwards, it's Johnathan from across the hall. May I come in?'

Still there was no reply. That was odd. Mr Edwards was usually home by this time – even if Johnathan hardly saw him, he couldn't miss the unmistakable sound of a kettle whistling when he passed his neighbour's apartment on the way to his own every evening.

Concerned that Mrs Higgins might harass them both even more than usual if he didn't at least try to give Mr Edwards fair warning about his rent, Johnathan tried once more. He might well have been knocking on the door of a wardrobe, for all the response he got. Wary of intruding upon his neighbour's privacy, he tried turning the handle. The door was unlocked, so he opened it a few inches to peer inside. He caught sight of stacks of open boxes, filled with notepads of varying shapes and sizes. 'What in Phlamel's name is that all about?' he whispered to himself, automatically using Alfred's old expression of the famed Alkemist, Nikoli Phlamel, who had first brought Alkemy to Nodnol.

On the few occasions that Johnathan had been in Mr Edwards' apartment, it had always been pristine and tidy to the point of being art. Never would he have expected to see such a haphazard assortment piled all over the place.

Curiosity overtaking him, he opened the door wider to get a better look. But what he saw shocked him so much that several choice curse words slipped from his mouth. Lying limply on the floor was Mr Edwards. If it wasn't for the slight rise and fall of his chest, Johnathan would have thought he was dead.

Rushing over, he took the man's hand. 'Mr Edwards, can you hear me?' He squeezed Mr Edwards' hand; there was a movement in the fingers in response. Good, at least he was somewhat conscious.

Dashing from the room and across to his own, Johnathan snatched up the bag that Alfred had given him and came back to kneel next to the poor man. Fishing through it, he found a powder labelled 'Essence of Wormkeel', a staple he knew Alfred would never have let him go without. Fetching a cup of water from the kitchen, he mixed the powder with it until it formed a light paste, and then applied some to Mr Edwards' upper lip, just under his nose. Within seconds, the man shuddered and opened his eyes.

'John ... Johnathan,' he said, weakly. Sweat ran down his brow, and his breathing was ragged.

'Mr Edwards, what happened to you?' Johnathan asked gently.

But Mr Edwards shook his head and pointed to the boxes. 'The Super Notes ... take ... them.' His eyes shut once more and his breathing slowed to a stop.

Johnathan's hands leapt to Mr Edwards' neck, searching for a pulse. There wasn't one. 'No!' Johnathan said under his breath. 'Come on, Mr Edwards!' He rooted through his bag again. Please let Alfred have put it in there!

His hands found a packet bulkier than most and as he pulled it out, he saw with satisfaction that it was what he was looking for. Golden Shellhorn, the most powerful single ingredient he knew of to shock a person's system into action. Taking one of the small golden pellets in his hand, he placed it under Mr Edwards' tongue and waited. Any second now, any second, and Mr Edwards' heart would start again. His lungs would take in fresh air ....

Johnathan waited for the Golden Shellhorn to take effect, but with each minute that passed, he knew that he had been a moment too late. He couldn't save Mr Edwards. His neighbour was gone forever.

Johnathan sat back from the body and buried his head in his hands. What had caused the man to collapse like that? He'd only been in his late forties, and as far as Johnathan knew from their brief encounters, had hardly ever needed to visit a Doktor or one of the Apothecaries. Johnathan just couldn't understand it.

He dried the streaks of tears from his face and looked at the boxes. Super Notes. That was what Mr Edwards had called the notepads inside them. He got up and went over to the nearest box. On the top of the pile, typed in neat lettering on marbled paper, was a flyer headed 'Super Notes: *the handy notepad that never lets you forget important appointments!*'. The flyer went on to detail three different types of Super Notes; ones that sang to you every so often so that you wouldn't forget what was on them, others that let off an alluring scent, and some that floated along behind you until whatever task or appointment was on them had been completed.

Johnathan grimaced. These sounded like an enchanted gimmick from a Wytch, and though he had never met one, he shared the common dislike for Wytches that all Alkemists had, for a Wytch could do naturally what an Alkemist might spend years trying to achieve, a thoroughly irritating fact of life. Fortunately, most people thought Wytches untrustworthy, for the simple reason that there was no explanation for how their powers worked. Alkemy, on the other hand, had a sound logic and required hours of study to perfect. However, it was not unknown for some in desperate situations (such as those with lifelong illnesses who believed that because a Wytch's powers were natural, any remedies made by them would be more effective than normal Alkemical-based medicines) to turn to one for help, and for the Wytch to oblige – for adequate payment, of course.

He read further down the flyer and realised it was a guide on how to sell them, with a full price list and tips to make customers interested. Had Mr Edwards truly planned on selling these?

Johnathan bit his lip. An idea had taken root in his mind that he didn't like, but given he was now jobless, he might not have any other choice. After all, Mr Edwards had begged him to 'take them' with his dying words. Would it really be such a terrible thing to try and sell them himself for a while, at least until he found another shop to take him on?

CHAPTER 2

*J*ohnathan fought against the shrill wind that was trying to force him backwards. He was knee-deep in snow, and every step was slow and measured so that he didn't fall off balance. Strung across his shoulder was the bag of ingredients that Alfred had left him and clutched in his hand was a case full of Super Notes, ready to be presented at the next household he stopped at.

A month had passed since Mr Edwards' death. Though Johnathan had called a Doktor to formally confirm it at the time, they hadn't been able to figure out why he'd died. Doktor Mannings had been most insistent that an autopsy be conducted, but Mrs Higgins wouldn't hear of it, saying that any such inquiries would delay her getting a tenant to replace him, and apparently, that was something she could ill afford. However, no sooner had Doktor Mannings signed the death certificate than two very important looking people came to see Mrs Higgins, and once they'd left, Johnathan saw her smiling – something he didn't think he'd ever caught her doing before.

It had taken every bit of Johnathan's self-control

not to ask what the visit was about, but at least he'd managed to hide the Super Notes in his own apartment before the people came back to take away the rest of Mr Edwards' belongings. Who they were was a mystery to him, and he was thoroughly irritated that Mrs Higgins hadn't even tried to contact any of Mr Edwards' relatives first, in case they would have liked his possessions. Still, Johnathan supposed it was no use being angry with her; the only thought she ever seemed to spare her tenants was whether they could pay her every month. There was no reason why she would change just because someone had died. And he knew if he ever dared to question her, she'd throw him out without giving him the chance to pack.

He sneezed violently as several snowflakes went up his nose. How he wished Boysenberry Lane wasn't so dreadfully steep. His legs were aching (what he could feel of them at least) and the houses perched in the distance seemed as far away as they had fifteen minutes ago.

Stopping for a moment, he blew on his hands and wriggled his fingers to help keep his circulation going. A stray newspaper billowed across his path, flapping around like an over-grown moth. In a flurry of ice and wind, it circled around in the air and then hit him full in the face. He pulled it away in agitation, about to tear it into shreds, but then his eyes caught the headline: Musical Bandits strike again; Family Devastated by Theft of Precious Jewellery Collection.

He frowned. There had been a lot of whispers about these so-called Musical Bandits throughout Nodnol over the past few weeks. It seemed that no one ever saw them; all they heard was a sweet, rhythmic music, and then their memories went blank.

'Musical indeed,' he muttered. 'Probably just some rogues who've stolen several bottles of Easy Draught to put everyone to sleep.' He tossed the paper roughly away into a nearby dustbin and picked up his bag and case again.

It was getting on for late afternoon; if he didn't reach those houses soon, he wouldn't have suitable daylight left to demonstrate the different qualities of the Super Notes, something he'd found invaluable when trying to sell them.

So far, he'd made well over six hundred Ren, more than enough to pay another two months' rent, giving him more time to look for a new shop to apprentice in and, boy, did he need it. He'd been to all the Alkemical Apothecaries in the city centre and none of them were interested in helping him. They all said that it would be too hard working with someone who already had their own way of doing things.

'And what *quaint* ways they are, indeed,' Alexander Benthas (one of the city's top Alkemical Apothecaries, despite being barely into his twenties) had said when Johnathan told him which shop he'd trained at.

Johnathan left in somewhat of a hurry shortly after, having *accidentally* upset Benthas' prize display of Angelic Resin. Benthas chased him halfway down the street with a mop reeking suspiciously of spoiled anti-fungal tonic - which was ironically made with an extremely potent forest fungus – but, fortunately, it had been market day and Johnathan managed to lose him in the crowd.

The memory made him snort, and with a new-found spurt of energy, he came to the top of Boysenberry Lane and the enormous houses that awaited him. Each one was easily as big as Johnathan's apartment building, fully detached, and with outer walls made of rough-shaped stone blocks. They looked impressive, and very, very expensive. The first one belonged to the Brewer family, who everyone knew owned Nodnol's best beer brewery. They were rumoured to have six children, and a very busy schedule. They were sure to be good candidates for the Super Notes.

Adjusting his coat and scarf and readying his case, Johnathan rang the doorbell. There was a slight delay and then the door opened to reveal the most harassed-looking butler that Johnathan had seen so far, and now that he was scouting the richer families, he had seen rather a lot.

'May I help you, sir?' the butler asked politely, but without a hint of a smile.

'Yes, good afternoon. My name is Johnathan Nesbit, seller of the bestselling Super Notes, and I've come to—'

'I'm terribly sorry, sir, but the Lady and Master are currently attending a party several doors down. I was assured that they would be out until late evening.'

'Ah,' Johnathan said, his enthusiasm suddenly extinguished. 'Perhaps you would be interested in buying some Super Notes yourself? They come in very handy when reminders are needed for what chores have to be done. Here,' he smiled, taking one of the pads of Super Notes from his case and holding it up. It was decorated with luminous musical notes. 'These ones sing to you if you haven't read them in a while. That's a rather pleasant way of jogging your memory, don't you think? And these—'

'Sir, I am sure that there are plenty of butlers and

maidservants out there who would benefit from such contraptions, but I assure you, *I* am not one of them. My memory is perfectly adequate and, if it weren't, then I certainly wouldn't be employed by such an esteemed family. Now, please, whilst I believe your intentions to be good, it would be best for you to leave the premises at once. Good evening!'

With that, he closed the door in Johnathan's face, leaving him standing on the doorstep like a statue. Well, Johnathan couldn't say it was the first time he'd received such rejection. In fact, a vast majority of the houses he went to shut him out after only a few words. 'On to the next house, then,' he muttered, and carried his bag and case with him through the gates and to the house opposite.

Sadly, the occupants of that house were also attending the party further down the street, as were the next and the next, until he reached the house at the very end. By this time the light had almost faded, but he could hear frivolities coming from inside. He had no doubt that this was where everyone was. Perhaps they would let him inside to warm his hands against their fire, and afterwards he could entertain them by making the Super Notes float and sing and make the room smell of sweet perfumes.

He stepped through the gates, about to head to the front door, when a large clump of snow fell off the roof and hit the dustbins stored along a side alley just inside the fence. They clanged richly, but the noise went unnoticed, hidden by the laughter and chatter from within.

Then someone giggled from outside the house. Johnathan looked around, but he couldn't see anyone.

'Shush, Chester, do you want someone to see us?'

It was a girl's voice, soft but with a definite touch of self-confidence.

'He's sorry, Jasmine, but he can't help himself every time he stands next to you. Your beauty just turns his legs to jelly. Isn't that right, Chess?' a boy asked gleefully.

'Shut up, Samuel! I lost my footing, that's all,' an older boy stated angrily.

'Be quiet, all three of you!' snapped a different girl, harsher than the first. 'Don't you dare breathe another word. Let's do our job and be out of here.'

'Oh, don't be so strict, Erin—'

'Samuel, if you don't pick up your flute right now and start playing, I'll box your ears!'

There was a sudden scrambling sound, and finally Johnathan was able to locate the speakers. Four dark shadows stood on the roof of the house, two girls and two boys, all slightly different heights. As quietly as he could, he stepped closer to the dustbins so he could get a better look. The Kerical street lights were flickering on now, and though he was hidden in shadow, the people on the roof suddenly became more visible.

The shortest one was a boy in his early teens, fitting together a silver flute, and next to him was a dark-haired girl, perhaps sixteen, who was making the boy on her other side, around the same age, blush so profusely that he kept having to look away. They both had string instruments, the girl a viola and the boy a violin. To their left, with a look of impatience on her face, was a girl of Johnathan's own age, whose green eyes reflected the Kerical lights so vividly that it looked like her pupils were filled with hidden fire.

She held a bodhran in her hands, and at her signal, the youngest boy began to play his flute.

The melody was lively and full, and soon the others joined in, creating an uplifting jig that called for Johnathan's feet to hop around in a dance. It penetrated every part of him, and even though he knew it couldn't have been any louder than the raucousness inside the house, it certainly felt like it was being performed by a full orchestra filling the whole street. He doubted that even the most befuddled guests would miss its call.

Quite abruptly, a wave of weariness crashed over him and he collapsed, clattering against the dustbins.

'Hey!'

Someone pushed hard on Johnathan's shoulders, shaking him awake. As his eyes opened, he found himself staring at a mouldy, decaying banana skin half buried by the snow. He rolled away from it and looked up. It was still night, and he was lying in the snow by the dustbins where he'd fallen.

'I said "Hey". You can't just ignore me!'

He blinked and shook his head before finally turning to the speaker. It was a girl of no more than twelve, with blonde hair in ringlets and blue eyes that stared at him accusingly. She was wearing a blue velvet dress with lace around the collar and cuffs.

'Who are you?' he asked without thinking. He could still hear chattering coming from inside the house, now mixed with the sound of someone attempting to play the piano, and had no idea what had made him faint so suddenly.

'What do you mean, who am I? I'm Molly Aqua, daughter of Lord and Lady Aqua, I'll have you know. Well, adopted daughter, but that still makes them my parents. The real question here is who are you, and why were you skulking around outside our house? I bet you were the one who did it. You were, weren't you? It must have been you, but I can't see Winkit anywhere.'

'Aqua ... the family who owns the hospital? And what in Nodnol is a Winkit? A pet, or something?' Johnathan asked, confused. Not only was he still dazed, but the cold was making his ears freeze.

'Winkit is far more than a pet, you stupid rat. She was my grandmother's cat, and my friend. Now tell me, what have you done with her?' the girl demanded imperiously.

'I haven't done anything with her. I haven't even *seen* a cat around here. I came to sell Super Notes, that's it. But I fainted ... I think.'

'Humph,' Molly said, crossing her arms. 'A likely story. I bet you snuck in here after hearing that silly tale that she's a Wytch's familiar. Well, I'll tell you, it's not true!'

'Why would I have any interest in a Wytch's familiar? I'm an Alkemist, we have an inherent dislike of Wytches,' he protested.

'Then why are those things in your bag so obviously enchanted by a Wytch? I had a look through that guide of yours, I know what abilities they have. Only a Wytch would be able to make a notepad that sings to you or floats by your head. Now, tell me how you did it and where you've hidden Winkit. What did you do to make us all fall asleep?'

'I'm telling you I – wait, did you say *everyone* else fell asleep too?' Something stirred at the back of his mind.

'Yes. Winkit was on my lap while I was sitting by

the fire, listening to mother and father talk to the guests. All of a sudden, I felt very tired, and then the next thing I knew, Winkit was gone and everyone else was picking themselves up off the floor saying that they'd all fallen asleep. They thought at first that maybe it was the Musical Bandits, but as nothing had been stolen, they passed it off as a bad batch of champagne. They wouldn't listen to me when I told them about Winkit; they said she'd only gone out to hunt mice. But she never does that. Not in the evening, at least.' She sniffed and rubbed her eyes, shivering.

Despite how cold he was, Johnathan found himself taking off his coat and putting it around her shoulders. 'Funny that you should mention the Musical Bandits,' he said after a while, 'because I saw some people up on your roof just before I collapsed. They had instruments with them and seemed quite eager to play.'

Molly looked up at him. 'You saw the Bandits? You actually *saw* them, and didn't think to *stop* them?'

'Well, I didn't know who they were and ...' he trailed off uncertainly. Who else would it have been? It wasn't as though people regularly hired musicians to play from their rooftops. Why *hadn't* he stopped them, or made his presence known?

'Never mind,' Molly snapped. 'You look useless anyway. You probably couldn't have scared them away if you'd tried. They're hardened criminals, after all.'

'Actually, they're just teenagers. The oldest one looks about my age, and I'm only seventeen,' he replied, trying not to be offended.

'Teenagers? What would they want with jewels and trinkets, and Winkit?'

'Who knows, but I've had enough of being questioned by you. I think I'll be off now, if you don't mind,' he said, picking up his things and taking his coat back from her.

'You can't just turn your back on me and walk away. You've *seen* the Bandits. No one *ever* sees the Bandits, but you did, and now you're going to help me look for them.'

'I – *what?*'

'You heard me. It's your fault they got away with it anyway, so come on, where do you think they went?' she said, scanning the ground for clues.

'Fine, let's think about this then. Do you see any footprints by the door, aside from your own?' he asked, unsure why he was getting involved. He didn't mind cats, but trudging around in the snow for them? Even if it *did* lead to finding a group of criminals, the whole idea was ludicrous.

She went to look, activating the porch light as she did so. 'Yes, there are. I think they belong to a boy. There's not much of an indent where the heel is, and it's more common for boys to have shoes with short heels than girls. They're also quite wide. Hold on a second; let me get my coat and a lantern from inside.'

Before he could say anything, she'd shrugged off his coat and darted through the sturdy oak door, reappearing moments later wearing her own ankle-length one and holding two Kerical lanterns. She gave him one and beckoned him over to where the footprints were. He examined them closely, noticing that there were two sets, side by side, one going into the house and one going out. There were no others aside from his own and Molly's. 'They go up this gap by the dustbins. He must have walked right past me while I was asleep,' he said.

Holding the lanterns high, they followed the footprints down the slight gap and around to the back of the house, where a long branch from an oak tree hung adjacent to it. 'At least we know how they got onto the roof in the first place,' he said. 'But how did they get out of the garden? The tree is on this side of the fence, and there aren't any gaps in the fence panels at all.'

'Don't be so sure of that,' Molly said, pulling him over to the left. The boy's footprints joined up with three others, disappearing a few feet away from where she and Johnathan were standing. She kicked the fence panel nearest, and to Johnathan's surprise, the top end swung forwards at an angle, leaving a gap at the bottom just big enough to wriggle through. He raised his eyebrow at her. She shrugged, and said simply, 'I get bored a lot being home-tutored. Sometimes I like to *explore* a bit between lessons.'

Johnathan found himself thinking that she might not be as stuck up as he thought.

CHAPTER 3

'*W*on't your parents worry that you're missing?' Johnathan inquired after they'd both wriggled through the gap in the fence and come out into a dark street on the other side. There were no Kerical lights here at all. Only a single, old fashioned gas lamp post stood before them, so worn with age that the black paint decorating it had all but flaked off. The timing mechanism inside it looked so rusty that even if they'd had a ladder, it would have been impossible to get it to light up.

'Of course not. My parents might not have big celebrations like this all the time, but when they do, their parties always go on past midnight, and they'll be so drunk by then that they won't notice I'm gone until the morning. Not even the maids will, because I always kick up a fuss when they check on me at night,' Molly explained.

'Oh,' he replied, holding his lantern high to try and figure out where they were. 'I don't recognise this street at all. I know we're at the back of Boysenberry Lane, but I'm sure I've never seen another street beside it. I thought it was all fields.'

'It is further down but, at one point, there were lots of streets back here. That was before the fire, though, about thirty years ago according to Mr Aster, my history tutor. Most people don't like to talk about it because so many families died, and they're still not completely sure what caused it, but it was right around the time that Kerical energy became so popular. He wouldn't have told me if I hadn't asked why only part of this street is here. This is all that's left. Not many people wanted to live here after that, which is why the developers decided to build houses up Boysenberry, to attract families back to the area,' she said.

'You mean Boysenberry Lane didn't exist back then?' Johnathan asked, stunned by this new information. The houses in Boysenberry looked so magnificent that he'd thought they were all old, period properties.

'No, all of the houses, including ours, were only built afterwards. My parents rent out the original Aqua House as an extra office for the Board of Alkemists. Mother says they pay handsomely for it.' She scanned the area. 'Enough questions, anyway. We've got to look for the Bandits. I bet Winkit's terrified by now.'

Johnathan caught sight of the footprints again as he examined the remnants of the street. They followed them for what seemed like miles, though the further they went, the harder it was to spot them because of how fast the snow was starting to fall. If they didn't catch up to the Bandits soon, they would lose the trail completely.

Though they had long since left the old street,

they still caught signs of burnt-out houses buried in the snow. With the wind whistling past their ears and only their lanterns guiding the way, both of them began to feel anxiety creep into their bones.

'How far do you think we've come?' Molly asked after they'd been silent for nearly an hour.

'It feels like three miles at least, but it's hard to tell when I can't see more than a few feet from my nose. I thought you knew this place, anyhow?' Johnathan questioned.

'I've never been up this far. Mostly I stay around the street, and sometimes the fields on the other side, but not here. It's too creepy. My tutor says they didn't even find all the bodies.'

Johnathan whipped around, aghast. 'Are you serious? There could still be *bodies* around here? What if we accidentally tread on one?'

'Don't tell me you're scared? You're five years older than me *and* you're a boy. If anyone's scared, it should be me!'

'Hey, dead bodies give lots of people the creeps; age and gender have nothing to do with it,' Johnathan said stiffly and trudged meaningfully onwards.

'Oh look, a sulking teenager. What an *unusual* sight,' she called behind him, running to catch up. Most of her words were lost by the wind, but Johnathan still caught the sarcasm.

'What would you know about it? You're nothing but a child, and a spoilt one at that! I've worked for three years as an apprentice Alkemical Apothecary, only to have my mentor diagnosed with Acute Energy Loss and be forced into closing his shop. My neighbour died the same day, for unknown reasons, and left me these Super Notes, which as you pointed out can only be enchanted by a Wytch, and you have *no idea* how ashamed I am that my sole source of income at the moment comes from selling them ... not to mention being rejected by nearly every Alkemical Apothecary in Nodnol. At this rate, I don't know if I'll *ever* be able to find somewhere to finish my apprenticeship!' he raged.

Molly looked at him, speechless. 'I'm sorry, I ... what's your name? I don't think you've told me yet.'

'It's Johnathan. And I think we've come to the end of the trail,' he said quietly. His sudden outburst had exhausted him; he hadn't realised just how angry he was about it all.

He looked up at the house that now stood before them, a solitary survivor among the ruins of its neighbours. Its brick exterior was charred and blackened, so much so that it looked like it might fall down at any second, and yet it stood without even a creak against the strong winds. If he listened closely, he thought he could hear the excited laughter of children from inside, too.

They edged closer, turning their lanterns down so that they had the bare minimum of light to see by. As they reached the front wall, the voices were unmistakable. Somehow, this house was *full* of children!

The windows and the doorway had been freshly boarded up; there was no trace of the fire on any of the planks, and light spilled through the gaps.

'There must be a way in. These planks are some kind of decoy from the real entrance,' he murmured, examining all four walls closely as they walked around the whole building. It wasn't a particularly small house, but it wasn't enormous either. He thought maybe four or five good-sized rooms at most, and the parts that weren't boarded up seemed mostly intact. 'I don't understand. They can't just appear in there. They have to be able to get in and out somehow.'

'You never learn, do you?' Molly said beside him, intensely studying the boarded-up doorway, focusing on the nails holding the planks shut. She pressed down hard on one of the planks and then let go. It sprang open on a hinge, along with four more, revealing a gap large enough to crouch through.

'I'm not even going to ask how you knew to do that,' Johnathan said, trying not to show how impressed he was. They went through, attempting to make as little noise as possible, and found themselves in a narrow hallway with two doors on the left and one on the right, and a warped set of stairs leading to a precarious looking second floor. At the far end, they could see what appeared to be a kitchen.

A dim Kerical light hung from the ceiling, illuminating the part of the hall closest to the doors. Treading lightly to try and stop the floorboards from creaking, Johnathan inched open the first door on the left. It was a spacious closet, and in it were four instrument cases. One for a violin, one for a viola, a round, soft case for a thin drum, and a long narrow case about the right size for a silver flute. There were also two hessian sacks filled with silver water jugs, trinket boxes, and jewellery. A smug grin settled on his face. He turned to tell Molly what he'd found, but she was looking past him into the kitchen, where a light had been switched on, and standing in the doorway was none other than the oldest girl from the roof of Molly's house. Her green eyes were even more

vivid up close, and her auburn hair neatly comple-
mented them. Her face was weary and drawn, but
there was no mistaking the fact that she really was
only Johnathan's age.

She stared at them in sheer horror as a half-black,
half-ginger cat came streaking forwards from
behind her.

'Winkit!' Molly cried. 'I'm so glad you're alright.'

'Well, of course she's alright,' the girl said, finally
finding her voice. It was as strict as Johnathan remembered it being. 'We would never harm her.'

'Then why did you take her? You *are* one of the
Musical Bandits, are you not?' Molly asked.

'Musical Bandits? I don't know what you—'

'Save it,' Johnathan said. 'I saw you on Molly's
roof a few hours ago, and we followed your footprints
all the way here. Not to mention I've just seen your
instruments in the closet.'

'Erin, what's taking so long? Where's the tea?'
The door on the right opened, and the head of the
youngest boy appeared from behind it. He took one
glance at her expression, however, and instantly
turned his head to see Johnathan and Molly. 'Intruders! How on earth did they get here?'

'*You* forgot to erase our tracks on the way back,
apparently. Our footprints were still visible,' Erin
replied, failing to conceal a sigh.

'Wait, I thought Chester and Jasmine were supposed to do that! I got the cat, after all,' the boy said
defensively.

'No, they were busy carrying our loot bags and
instruments. And you only retrieved Winkit from the
house, I was the one who carried her back here. You
know that whoever has free hands has to do it. You're

lucky our guests aren't the police ... though those bungling fools are far too occupied playing teacher's pet with the Board of Alkemists to care much about us.' She turned to Johnathan and Molly. 'I am curious, though. How did you find your way into this house?'

'We walked in the front door, actually,' Johnathan replied.

Next to him, the boy came fully out into the hall, followed by the remaining two Bandits, who looked as shocked as Erin had been. Now that he saw them in full light, he noticed that both the boys had similar pale skin and hair, while the girl had a darker, chestnut complexion, with long, ebony hair.

'How did you know how to open it?' the older boy asked, scratching his freckled face. 'We're the only ones who know the trick to it.'

'No, you're not,' Molly said with a flick of her blonde ringlets. 'I have the same catch on one of my wardrobes. All I had to do was take a good look at those nails. I could tell straight away that they didn't really hold the wood together.'

'This is all beside the point,' Erin said flatly, holding a hand up to the others to quiet them. 'Let's go into the other room and we can discuss exactly why you followed us and what we can do for you. Quietly now, I've only just put the others to bed.'

She gathered a tray of cups and a pot of tea from the kitchen and led everyone into the room on the right. It was filled with faded, floral armchairs and neatly folded blankets. There was an old fireplace in one corner but, due to the state of the building's foundation, it had been, quite sensibly to Johnathan's mind, cordoned off. A neat coffee table took the centre, with a half-played game of chess displayed on its surface, which Erin moved aside to make space for the tray.

She gestured for Molly and Johnathan to sit down. They did so, taking separate armchairs that faced the seats where the Bandits took position. Winkit had jumped up onto Molly's lap and was now purring contentedly, though every so often Johnathan thought he caught her glaring at the younger boy.

'Seeing as you already know our secret, let us introduce ourselves. This is Samuel,' Erin said, indicating the boy, 'and his brother, Chester,' she continued, turning to the older one. 'Then we have Jasmine—'

Jasmine gave a slight curtsey, making both Johnathan and Chester blush even more, to which Molly reacted by leaning over to stamp on Johnathan's foot.

'And finally myself. My name is Erin Stronghold. Together, we are what *you* call the "Musical Bandits". But to the few children we look after here, we are their guardians and friends.'

'I'm sorry, but did you say your name was Erin *Stronghold*? As in the Stronghold family who co-founded the Board of Alkemists two hundred years ago?' Johnathan choked.

'Unfortunately, yes. But after my parents tried to force me into an arranged marriage last year, I try not to associate with them too much. I only sneak over to their house when I need to catch up on what Father is up to. So far, they haven't caught me,' she replied with a wry smile. 'Now, if you don't mind, who are you?'

'My name is Johnathan Nesbit, and I am - or was, I'm not sure now - an Alkemical Apothecary apprentice. My mentor became sick recently and had to close his shop, so now I'm having to get by using other ... means,' he said awkwardly.

Jasmine looked at him curiously. 'By theft?' she asked as though she approved.

'No, nothing like that,' he said quickly. 'I sell Super Notes; they're supposed to help you remember important engagements and things.'

'Oh,' Jasmine said, clearly disappointed. She turned to Molly. 'What about you?'

But it was Samuel who answered. 'She's the brat from the Aqua house who had Winkit on her lap. You have no idea how hard it was not to wake her even with you lot still playing. Twitchy one, she is.'

'Twitchy?! I'll give you twitchy, you slimy cat-thief!' Molly said with such a poisonous look that it might have killed a well-tended lawn.

'Calm down, Miss Aqua,' Erin said softly. 'We only took Winkit because we needed her help. You must know by now that she's a Wytch's familiar—'

'No, she isn't! It's just a stupid rumour going around,' Molly snapped, jumping up so suddenly that Winkit fell from her lap onto the floor. She hissed and sauntered over to Johnathan's case, sniffing at the Super Notes with interest.

'Rubbish, you little snot!' Samuel spat back at her. 'I may not be a Wytch myself, but there's plenty of Wytch-blood in my family, and I was born with the ability to recognise Wytch's familiars. I'm telling you, she's one of them.'

'*Alright*, Samuel, that's enough!' Erin said, bringing her hands together in a sharp clap. From outside the door there came a giggling. She glanced sideways and the giggling stopped abruptly. 'Now you've woken the children up. Listen, Miss Aqua, Winkit belonged to your grandmother, Mrs Irene Aqua, did she not?'

'Yes,' Molly said. 'Grandmother had Winkit from a kitten. But I don't see how—'

'And how old was your grandmother when she got Winkit?' Erin pressed.

Molly thought for a moment. 'She was thirteen, I think.'

'Then, given that the average lifespan for a normal cat is ten to fifteen years, and your grandmother died at the age of eighty only last year, wouldn't you conclude that Winkit has lived an extraordinarily long time? Not to mention that thirteen is the age when a Wytch fully comes into her powers and is normally bonded with a familiar upon her birthday.'

'But ... but Winkit is a special breed *known* for their long lifespan. Grandmother told me.'

'Did she happen to mention the name of the breed?' Erin asked with a trim smile.

'Well, no, she didn't, but I'm sure if you ask any breeder in Nodnol, they'd tell you,' Molly replied.

'I did, the first time I saw Winkit, back when I was a child. I'd never seen a cat with fur a different colour on each side, and I'd always wanted a kitten of my own, despite knowing that my parents would never have allowed it. Yet none of the breeders I spoke to knew of a breed that matched Winkit. So I began to believe the rumours about her. And when Samuel saw her a few weeks ago, meeting in an alley with a group of other cats, he confirmed it.'

'If that's the case, then he's definitely lying. Winkit would never meet with common, dirty cats.

Besides, everyone knows that a Wytch's familiar always speaks,' Molly said primly.

'Indeed, they do,' Erin said. She turned to Winkit. 'Would you care to oblige us?'

Winkit looked back at her sourly and then, in a voice that sounded as though it was still stiff from lack of use, said, 'Very well, I can see this argument has gone on long enough.'

Molly slid off her chair in surprise, but Winkit ignored her. Instead, she turned to Johnathan. 'Those Super Notes, or whatever you call them. How do you think they work?'

Johnathan blinked at her. 'I, uh, presumed they were enchanted by a Wytch.'

Winkit licked her front paws. 'Wrong,' she said finally. 'They haven't been touched by a Wytch – at least not in the normal way. No, I feel these are something entirely different, and I'm not so sure they're safe.'

'What do you mean? They're just notepads,' Johnathan replied, furrowing his brow.

'On the surface, they do appear that way,' Winkit agreed. 'But I feel that this is not their true form. I find it hard to explain, but they have an aura coming from them. If I were not used to such things, it would have me retching.' She flicked a whole Super Note pad out of the case with a deft swipe of her paw. 'If I were you, I'd see what happens when you burn one. Here, I'll do it for you. Pass me your Kerical lantern.'

Johnathan did so while the others watched on, equally curious. Hooking a claw onto the small hinged door that would expose the lantern's controlled flame, she opened it and nudged the edge of the Super Note inside with her nose. It took a few seconds to catch, but when it did, an almighty, piercing scream lurched through the entire room, coming from the Super Note itself.

Everyone glanced at each other. Whatever they'd been expecting, it certainly wasn't that.

CHAPTER 4

*G*reen tendrils of smoke oozed out from the smouldering remains of the Super Note, curling around their ankles. Then it gathered together, forming a dense shape directly above the Super Note itself. Arms, legs, torso, and finally a head; the image wavered as the group drew in their breaths sharply.

It was a woman, middle-aged and dressed in what looked like a prison uniform. She held her head down and her hands were handcuffed in front of her. For a few seconds, further details, such as her bobbed hair-style and broken nose became clearer, but then the image fell apart to become nothing but smoke once more.

'What ...was that?' Johnathan asked Winkit, who had been eyeing the apparition with deep suspicion in her almond-shaped eyes.

'I'm not certain,' she replied, swishing her tail, 'but it reminds me of a rumour I heard many years ago. Tell me, have any of you ever heard of something called a Nekromancer?'

Johnathan and the Musical Bandits shook their

heads, but Molly looked at her with sudden apprehension. 'Grandmother used to tell me stories sometimes when I was little, before Mother and Father found out and stopped her. They didn't think stories of Wytches were suitable for my education. One of them was about a Wytch who became interested in the workings of Alkemy. She said that this Wytch realised that Alkemy could make things possible that she had never dared believe; things like controlling a person, and even bringing them back from the dead. For many years the Wytch carried out her studies in secret, but eventually, because the smell of the bodies she'd been collecting for her experiments drifted into the streets, the police and the Board of Alkemists discovered what she was up to and had her imprisoned for life. She died there but, before she did, she began referring to herself not as a Wytch, but as a Nekromancer,' she said, shivering slightly.

'Ah, so she did tell you,' Winkit said approvingly. 'Yes, a Nekromancer is a person who strives to bring back the dead, and not just so they can see their loved ones again, but so they can control them and force them to do their bidding. Nekromancers, like the one in the story, are often Wytches, but there have been a few throughout the ages who strived to achieve results with Alkemy alone.'

'You mean, there really are people trying to do this? Nekromancers *actually* exist?' Molly said, shocked. 'I thought it was just a story.'

'Many stories have a truth to them, Molly. Fortunately, the Nekromancer in your story and the many who followed were never actually successful in their experiments. But after seeing our smoky friend here, I'm beginning to wonder if one finally has succeeded.'

'Wait a second, Winkit,' Erin said, still staring at the remains of the Super Note. She had a haunted look on her face, and her usual severity had been stripped away. To Johnathan, she seemed scared and vulnerable. 'What we saw just now wasn't a real person who'd been brought back; it was just an image, a trick, surely?'

'That's what I wish to determine, Erin. Until we find more information, all I can do is speculate, but I think it is safe to say that someone, somewhere, is up to no good. And it would not surprise me if this was somehow linked to your concerns, too,' Winkit replied solemnly.

Erin swallowed and exchanged glances with Samuel, Chester and Jasmine. They all looked as worried as she did. 'I think I'm missing something here,' Johnathan whispered to Molly. She inclined her head. 'I don't suppose you'd mind telling us what's really going on here?' he requested of them.

'Yes, you still haven't told us properly why you needed Winkit,' Molly pointed out. 'You said you needed her help. What kind of help?'

'What do you know about Acute Energy Loss, Johnathan?' Jasmine asked him. 'After all, if you're an Alkemical Apothecary apprentice, you should have heard of it by now.'

'It's a rare disease with no cure that causes people such dreadful fatigue that they eventually become bedridden. It's usually only diagnosed within the elderly and most die from it. My mentor, Alfred, has it. He sent me a letter last week saying he was moving to the country to spend his last few months with his daughter,' he offered, a lump forming in his throat at the thought of never seeing the old man again.

'I see,' Jasmine said. 'Well, you're nearly right. But the fact is, there have now been ten cases of it affecting entire households, including teenagers and young children, within this past month. And we're not talking poor families who might not have access to proper medical treatment. These are rich households with their own private Doktors.'

'So, what are you saying?' he asked. 'I mean, this is serious, of course, but why should it concern you?'

'This isn't just serious, Johnathan; something is really wrong here! How many cases are there usually of Acute Energy Loss? Maybe five or six per year? Don't you think it's suspicious that suddenly there's nearly fifty in a month?' Erin questioned, her voice trembling.

'You think someone's making this happen deliberately?' he queried. 'How?'

'That's what we're trying to find out,' Chester broke in. He had been so silent that Johnathan had forgotten he was there. 'We want to make sure that whatever's causing it, it won't affect the kids we look after. And because Winkit is still in contact with other Wytches' familiars, we wondered if she knew anything about it. We thought perhaps it was the work of a rogue Wytch.'

'And as I was about to explain to Erin before the two of you joined us,' Winkit said to Johnathan and Molly, 'the fact is that no one knows what the cause is. If it is a Wytch, then it's either one from outside Nodnol, or one who's awoken prematurely and doesn't have a familiar yet. However, the more I ponder it, the less this being a Wytch's work seems likely.' She went over to Johnathan and jumped up onto his lap, looking at him directly. 'Tell me something: where exactly did those Super Notes come from?'

'Er, they were my neighbour's. He died suddenly and left them to me. There are boxes of them,' he told her.

'What did he die of, do you know?'

He shook his head. 'The Doktor who came to examine him wanted to do an autopsy, but our landlady didn't want anything delaying his funeral so that she could rent his apartment out to someone else. There was something strange, though. Two official-looking people came to see her and, after that, all trace of his belongings disappeared ... apart from the Notes, which I'd already moved into my own apartment. But I was the one who found him, and he was still alive when I got there. He'd collapsed on the floor by the boxes of Super Notes, and when I used my powders to help him regain consciousness, he only pointed and told me to take them. He slipped away after that, and even though I used Golden Shellhorn, I couldn't save him.'

'Now that *is* interesting,' Winkit mused aloud. 'What was your neighbour's name, by chance?'

'Mr Edwards. I think his first name was Renaldo.'

Erin gasped. 'Renaldo Edwards? Oh, no ... I knew there was a reason I hadn't seen him lately. But to think that he was dead ...'

'You knew him, Erin?' Johnathan asked, as surprised as everyone else in the room.

'Yes, I did. He was a researcher for the Board of Alkemists. I first met him when I was a child on an inspection of the research facility by my parents, but every now and then when my governess took me out on walks, I'd catch him wandering about Nodnol in a shabby suit and carrying his briefcase, and I'd ask him what he was up to. I didn't understand then that Father had forbidden all his staff to talk about their work, so when Renaldo evaded my questions, I became quite persistent. Eventually, he started giving me hints – he was just looking for something – such as there'd been a Lectric storm and he needed to speak with the engineers checking the powerlines, or he had a meeting with an ingredient trader, that kind of thing. It turned into a game. Then Father found out and even though I still saw him roaming the city, he kept his mouth shut other than to say hello.'

Johnathan gaped at Erin, speechless. For the three years he'd lived next to Mr Edwards, he'd thought he was a simple door-to-door salesman, when in fact he'd worked for the Board of Alkemists! Johnathan could have kicked himself for how many wasted opportunities and deep conversations there might have been between them.

Winkit flicked her tail, accidentally hitting Johnathan on the cheek. 'Hmm,' she said. 'I think we had better look at those boxes of Super Notes you have. I want to find out where they came from, and exactly what they are.'

∼

Johnathan woke bleary-eyed and dazed. He didn't know what time he'd returned home the previous night, but it felt like he hadn't rested at all. He remembered having to drag Molly back to her house after Winkit had ordered her to go home, cold, tired and with wet trouser bottoms because the snow had gone from crunchy powder to icy sludge. Winkit herself had decided to stay with the Bandits until the morning, when they would all be coming to Johnathan's apartment to examine the boxes. They'd had to arrange a time when Mrs Higgins would be out, because Johnathan was sure there would be no end of trouble if she found anyone in the building who didn't belong. Over the years he'd lived there, he had noticed that she made a habit of going to the mid-morning market, so if they visited at that time, the coast would hopefully be clear.

Outside his door came a banging sound, and then the shuffling of a clumsy pair of feet. Curious, Johnathan dragged himself from the bed and threw on his waffled dressing gown. His Kerical alarm clock only read eight forty-five, far too early for the Bandits to arrive. Besides, he had given them strict orders to wait on the corner of the street for him, just in case there were any delays with Mrs Higgins' departure.

He shuffled over to the door and unlocked it, peering out through a small gap. He caught glimpses of someone – a very large, rotund someone – heaving piles of suitcases and boxes into Mr Edwards' old apartment. The man, for now he saw flashes of a large black moustache and well-groomed beard, wheezed as he pushed and pulled, trying to get an awkwardly shaped trunk through the doorway.

Eventually, after watching his new neighbour sweat and curse, Johnathan felt so sorry for him that he opened his door wide and offered to help. 'Good morning, sir,' he said, making the man jump and hit his head on the doorframe in surprise. 'May I be of assistance?'

The man beamed at him as though he was some kind of hero. 'I wouldn't mind a hand with the rest of my belongings. I admit I'm not quite as fit as I once was, and I'd rather not kill myself by simply trying to move in. Humphrey's my name, Kerical engineering's my game.' He extended a sweaty hand to Johnathan.

Johnathan took it cautiously, his eyes widening at the strength of Humphrey's grip. 'I'm Johnathan.' He took back his hand and massaged it. 'Er, let's see if we can shift this trunk then, shall we?'

With their combined efforts, and after some scrambling, the trunk managed to fit through the door. Just as Johnathan was about to say good luck and go back into his own apartment, however, Humphrey revealed that he had ten more suitcases and nearly as many boxes to bring up from the hall below. By the time they were finished, they were both utterly exhausted with their stomachs grumbling.

'The Bandits!' Johnathan suddenly thought as he caught sight of the clock on Humphrey's wall, which read half past ten. He wasn't even dressed yet, let alone ready to go and meet them.

In a mad scramble, he mumbled his goodbyes to Humphrey and dashed back into his own apartment. He washed hastily, throwing on a crumpled shirt, trousers, slip-on shoes and an old coat, and then hurtled downstairs so fast that he slid down the last few steps, landing on his rear with a thump.

Quickly, he put his ear to Mrs Higgins' door to make sure she'd definitely left the building. There was silence from inside, confirming her absence, for when she was home, she always had her gramophone on, playing music even more ancient that she was.

Johnathan left the building and strode to the end of the street, trying to stay as casual as if he was just out for a midday stroll. Unfortunately, he hadn't counted on the ice that had formed from the slush of snow during the night. His feet skidded out from under him, causing him to walk with his arms splayed out for balance. When he reached the corner where the Bandits and Winkit were waiting, he found Jasmine and Samuel in fits of giggles.

'What happened to *you*?' Jasmine asked, making Johnathan feel terribly self-conscious. 'You look as though you were attacked by a violent washcloth while attempting to dress yourself in the dark.' She took out a small compact from the pockets of her thick coat and opened it so he could see his reflection in its small mirror.

His face, where he'd scrubbed rapidly, was covered in red blotches and the buttons on his shirt, visible where his coat hung open, were done up wrong. He saw his face redden even more with embarrassment before she finally shut the compact again.

'And what was up with your walk? It was like you were trying to be an ice skater,' Samuel said, still laughing, 'and your balance is even worse than Chester's!'

'Shut up, Sam!' Chester spat as his brother pulled a face at him. Jasmine was smirking at him too, and he had to turn away from her.

Erin rolled her eyes at the three of them. She looked back at Johnathan as Winkit decided to jump up into his arms and then climb painfully onto his shoulder, claws out for balance. 'Is your landlady out as you said she would be?' she asked.

'Yes, I just checked. I did have a new neighbour move in today, into Mr Edwards' old apartment, but I don't think he'll mind if I have company,' he answered, wincing as Winkit adjusted her grip.

'Very well then. Lead the way, I'm half-frozen out here.'

Johnathan led them inside and up the stairs to his apartment. Humphrey was busy unpacking as they went past and didn't even notice them. Inside his apartment once more, Johnathan locked the door behind them.

The boxes of Super Notes were all stacked in one corner. He and Chester pulled them into the middle of the room and, after throwing off their coats, everyone began taking out the Super Notes to examine.

Some of the boxes were still unopened and it was these that Winkit took the most interest in. 'Look here,' she called after a moment, tapping her paw on the flap of paper where the delivery address was printed.

Erin read it with interest. 'Well, I can't say I'm surprised. Renaldo wouldn't have ordered these himself. I wonder how he found out about them though. Until I saw Johnathan's, I'd never even heard of Super Notes.'

'What is it?' Johnathan asked, scanning the address himself. The package was addressed to a Mr James Phelby of Horace Close. How had he not noticed that before? He had moved them into his apartment rather quickly, he supposed, and the labels *were* mostly facing the wall ...

A terrible thought crossed Johnathan's mind. If Mr Edwards hadn't really been a salesman, then perhaps when he'd asked Johnathan to take the Super Notes, he wasn't asking him to sell them, but to keep them safe for some reason. 'Erin ...what are the names of the main families affected by Acute Energy Loss?'

'Let me think. The Eclaire family ... the Scarrows, Farmborrows, Templars, Anstroms, Deverish, Panthos, Eddings, Phillys and ...' She pulled a face. 'The last one escapes me.'

Johnathan had turned white as a sheet. 'It wasn't the Hoverrums, was it?'

'Yes, I think it was. Johnathan? Johnathan, what's wrong?'

But Johnathan couldn't hear her. He'd collapsed on the floor in a faint.

CHAPTER 5

a fizzing sound filled Johnathan's ears and he awoke to find Erin holding out a glass containing a hazy liquid, with bubbles rushing to the top.

'What is that?' he asked with effort.

'Something to make you feel better. I used the ingredients in your bag,' she replied as he took the concoction from her. 'You've got lots of interesting things in there. I never expected whole Gradda roots, or Pin's Pyrite.'

'It all came from the shop I worked at. My mentor, Alfred, managed to save it from the research facility. They sent a motor carriage to collect our apparatus and main ingredient stock,' he explained bitterly and took a sip of Erin's potion, swirling it around in his mouth to see if he could detect what she'd put in it. He smiled. 'Foster Lynch, Ansillium and Woodhide. Classic calming and replenishment ingredients.'

'Very good,' Erin said approvingly. 'So, you *do* know your stuff.'

'Of course I do, but I admit I'm surprised that you know it, too,' Johnathan said, drinking the rest of it

down. He put the glass onto the table next to him, realising that they'd lifted him onto the sofa.

'Really? You know very well how respected my
family is in the Alkemy world. I may not like *them*,
but I've always been interested in basic Alkemy. I
would have pursued it with my studies, had I been
able to choose what form most interested me. Unfortunately, they all interest me in some way.' She sat
down next to him, smoothing her dress. 'So, what
shocked you so much that you decided to take a nap
on the floor?'

The others were still busy checking the Super
Notes for any clues as to their origin or what they really were. Johnathan was glad, because Erin was more
level-headed than they were and unlikely to rebuke
him too harshly. He took a breath, trying to find the
words. 'When you mentioned the names of the families, I remembered that every one of them had
brought Super Notes from me, and not just one or
two pads, but many. Each of those families has lots of
children and the parents, and sometimes the maids
and butlers, found it was rather difficult keeping their
schedules in order and remembering important occasions. When I demonstrated what the Super Notes
could do to remind them, they jumped at the idea. I
sold to all of them within this last month – a whole
box full, altogether.'

'Which directly corresponds to when they were
diagnosed with Acute Energy Loss,' she said, suddenly understanding. 'Winkit could be right then.
Maybe these Super Notes are linked to the illness.
But how? Even if they're not what they seem to be,
how could they cause a disease like that to develop?'

They both thought for a moment, but they simply couldn't come up with anything.

There was a crash as one of the boxes toppled over, barely missing Winkit. The Super Notes inside spilled out, revealing the box's empty base. Something was stamped on it and as Johnathan and Erin joined the others to have a look, they saw it was a symbol of a set of simple scales with a black circle above one side and a white circle above the other.

'What does *that* mean?' Chester asked, puzzled. 'I've never seen that mark before.' He passed his thumb over it and then drew it back, sniffing the ink stain now on his skin. 'It's definitely Nodnol ink,' he told them. Johnathan gave him a questioning look. 'Our parents were Inkers before they died. Sam was too young to learn any of the trade, but I was able to pick up a few bits. Every company in Nodnol has a specific blend of ink for their trademark stamps. The ingredients are always the same, but the quantity of each is what makes them unique. Any inks from outside Nodnol use different ingredients, so that's why I'm so sure this one was made here in the city. It has the same subtle, yet distinctive smell as the ones we used to make.'

'So, can we use the ink to find out what Inker shop it comes from, and then who their client is?' Johnathan asked quickly.

Chester shook his head. 'Unfortunately, it's not that simple. There are over a hundred Inker shops in Nodnol. The biggest ones only serve the most prosperous companies, but the smaller shops mix ink for any sort of business, as long as they can pay. It would take us months to make any headway. All I can say is that the Inker had some skill, because the smell of the ink hasn't transferred to the Super Notes. It's stayed within the ink itself, and that's very hard to achieve.'

Johnathan sighed. 'I guess we're just going to have to find the answers somewhere else. Curse Mrs Higgins! She let those people take Mr Edwards' belongings off so quickly after he died. He might have kept a diary or a workbook that had the answer.'

'Wait a moment!' Erin said, snapping her fingers. 'He *would* have kept a diary, and written reports about everything he'd found. I'm sure he'd have kept them at the research facility, where they wouldn't get lost or tampered with!'

Everyone looked at her stupidly. 'But Erin, that just gives us another problem,' Jasmine pointed out. 'If they're at the research facility, how are *we* going to get to them? You've told us how dangerous some of the stuff is that they're developing in there; they won't even let reporters in past the reception area. It's not as though we can just waltz in and ask to see Mr Edwards' work. And you know we'd be far too visible to use our instruments to put them to sleep.'

'Actually, we *can* just walk in, assuming we have the proper *paperwork*.' The usual severity in Erin's expression replaced itself with one of pure mischief. 'Do you have a typewriter, Johnathan? Preferably with fresh ribbons?'

Unsure if it was wise, Johnathan went over to his desk and opened the largest drawer, bringing out a well-used typewriter given to him by Alfred the first week of his apprenticeship, all those years ago. He checked the condition of the ribbons and then took out some typing paper and secured it in place before taking the whole thing over to Erin.

'Excellent,' she said and for the next ten minutes,

while Johnathan brought round tea and biscuits, she sat typing as though nothing else mattered, occasionally stopping to tear out the paper and crumple it up, and starting again on a fresh sheet. When she had finished, she snatched the paper out and showed it to them. It read:

Dear Mr Murston,

It has come to my attention that the Alkemic Research Facility is overdue for inspection. Although I understand that this is short notice, I request that you allow my inspection team access to all areas of the facility. I have no doubt that the facility is running smoothly and no issues have arisen; however, as my team must make a full report, I expect your complete co-operation with any questions they may have.

Yours faithfully,
Arthur Stronghold,

Director in Chief of the Board of Alkemists

Johnathan choked as he finished reading. 'You're planning to get us in using that? A lie under your father's name?'

Erin shrugged. 'Why not? All it needs now is his signature at the bottom, and I've been able to forge that for years.'

Samuel smirked and murmured, 'That's our Erin.'

'Oh, come on, this will never work,' Johnathan protested. 'How can you be so sure that they haven't had an inspection already? It'll be awfully suspicious if they have two so close together. And we're all young; we don't look anything like inspectors. What if they recognise you, Erin?'

'Johnathan, I may have little personal contact with my family, but don't think for one moment that I'm not interested in what they're up to. I've kept a close eye on the goings on at the facility; they haven't had an inspection for over a year, ever since they made a breakthrough in Kerical wave transmissions. Father's been so wrapped up with it that something as trifling as an inspection hasn't even entered his mind. It's the perfect opportunity!' she declared.

'Alright, even if the letter's fine, what about our appearance?' he retorted.

In answer, Erin looked at Jasmine. Jasmine stared back, her face rigid, but Erin's expression was so sincere that she couldn't help but give in. 'Fine, I'll speak to Mother. Perhaps the laundrette can *misplace* a few suits this week. But you'll owe me. I don't want to be in charge of any of the children's bath times from now on. You know I hate it. It's bad enough having to drag out that tin bath and boiling the water for it for my own bathing.'

'Done,' Erin said. 'Let's get going.'

～

They arrived at the laundrette in Brocker Street twenty minutes later. It was a cramped, ragged shop squeezed between an enormous motor carriage workshop and a designer Kerical lamp shop.

Johnathan had only been up Brocker Street a few times before and like the ones in front of them now, it was truly a mishmash of businesses. It was very popular with shoppers, especially those visiting from outside the city, because there was always more to look at than there first appeared. On every visit, new shops selling eclectic items were to be discovered, and two of Nodnol's most famous spas resided there, one at each end.

Jasmine led the way into the dingy launderette. A bell rang as she opened the door, and a woman appeared with a face so decorated with make-up that she resembled a porcelain doll, taking her place behind the counter to greet them. However, when she saw Jasmine, the over-enthusiastic smile dropped from her face as though she'd suddenly taken a bite from a sour fruit.

'Oh, it's you,' she said, her tone flat.

'It's nice to see you too, Mother,' Jasmine replied. 'We need a favour.'

Her mother snorted so violently that Johnathan flinched. 'I don't do favours, Jasmine. I make bargains. If there's something you want, I expect to be paid a fee for it.'

Jasmine seemed to have anticipated this, for out of her coat pocket she drew a necklace of what looked like pearls and a moonstone. 'What do you think of this?' she asked, holding it out for her mother to see.

With deft hands, her mother snatched it from her and, pulling a magnifying glass from her blouse pocket, examined the necklace with great care. 'Callos pearls. The real deal,' she muttered, 'and a spiral moonstone, no less. Not bad, not bad at all.' She looked up at Jasmine. 'Where did you get this?'

'I acquired it from a rather rich lady last week – using your old trick of sleight of hand while I helped her gather the groceries she'd dropped. I've been meaning to trade it in for Ren at the usual place, but if it's up to your standards, I'll give it to you instead,' Jasmine replied smugly.

Her mother put the magnifying glass away and put the necklace around her bony neck. 'Alright,' she said seriously. 'What do you want?'

'We need suits. Posh ones. Three of them for the boys, and two formal skirts and blouses for Erin and me. Oh, and if you have any of those white lab coats, five of those too,' Jasmine said, looking to Erin for confirmation. She inclined her head.

'Anything for the cat?' Jasmine's mother said sarcastically, seeing Winkit jump up onto Johnathan's shoulder once more.

'A small bowl of milk, if it's not too much trouble,' Winkit replied, amused as Jasmine's mother gasped and fled into the back room.

'I thought you didn't want anyone finding out that you're a familiar?' Johnathan asked her.

'I don't particularly, but sometimes when I see irritating humans, it is fun to surprise them,' she replied, licking her paw to clean behind her ears.

The square Kerical washing devices lining the walls hummed and whirred while they waited. It had been a long time since Johnathan had seen any, preferring to do his own laundry by hand and then hanging it on the curtain pole over the bathtub. Each device had a glass door that swung open to reveal a cylindrical drum where dirty washing could be placed, and on the top were rows of buttons to press and knobs to turn, depending on what the item of clothing being washed was made from and the desired finish. Not only would they wash the clothes, but they could de-bobble, iron, tie-dye and, when used with certain Alkemical washing powders (which were twice as much Ren as the normal ones), could change the very make-up of the fabric into something else until its next wash.

After a few minutes, Jasmine's mother came back, pushing a rack of freshly pressed clothes. She handed out three tailored suits to Johnathan, Chester and Samuel, and as requested, a skirt and blouse each for Erin and Jasmine. She then went to the front door and turned the sign from 'open' to 'closed', and ushered the girls into the back room with her, leaving the boys to get changed where they were.

As Johnathan slipped on the trousers and crisp, white shirt – a far whiter white that his own shirt had been – he noticed that they smelled faintly of citrus fruits. The jacket carried it as well and as he put it on, it slid snugly over his shoulders, a perfect fit. There was even a tie in the top pocket that matched the suit's colour and, using his reflection in one of the glass doors of an empty washing device, he tied it around his neck. When he was done, he turned around to see that Chester and Samuel's suits and ties were identical to his own, and also fit well.

'She may be an unusual lady,' Samuel said, tucking in his shirt, 'but she's never let us down yet, has she, Chess? You remember when she let Jasmine borrow that lace gown to get into the masked ball last spring? She looked so pretty that you walked head-long into a Kerical lamp post trying to wave to her from across the street.'

Chester rounded on him. 'Sam, if you say one more thing about me and Jasmine, I'll—'

'Mumble and walk away?' Jasmine offered,

coming back into the room, followed by her mother and Erin.

Chester flushed and turned his back on her. Jasmine chuckled. She was carrying the white lab coats they needed and her mother was holding a spotted bag that bulged at the sides.

'Now that you're all dressed, I suppose I'd better get on with the important part,' Jasmine's mother said. She undid the bag, taking out various pots and tubes, an assortment of brushes and what looked like a mass of various-coloured fur.

'What ... is that?' Johnathan asked warily.

'Make-up,' Jasmine's mother replied curtly.

'Come off it ... we don't need any of that,' Samuel said, repulsed.

'Oh really? You seriously expect the research facility to let in a bunch of teenagers after reading one dubious little note? I don't think so, short stuff. In fact,' she said, eyeing him up, 'I may have to find some inserts for your shoes to make you look taller. Honestly, I don't think you've grown an inch in the two years I've known you.'

'Hey!'

'Quiet, Sam,' Erin chided. 'She knows what she's doing.'

'Right,' Jasmine's mother said. 'Who's first? Come on, I don't have all day.'

After an hour, the five of them were ready to go. Jasmine and Erin had dark makeup on with a few fake laughter lines around their mouths, as well as dark circles under their eyes to make them look older and more worn. Johnathan, Chester and Samuel, however, had much more extensive makeovers. Johnathan sported a short black beard and trim moustache to go with his hair, Chester had sideburns and thickened eyebrows, and Samuel – as well as having inserts in his shoes as Jasmine's mother had threatened – was decorated with a moustache, thick eyebrows, sideburns, *and* a pair of spectacles.

The effect was dramatic. All of them now appeared to be in their late thirties and, with their lab coats on, every inch an inspector as the ones Johnathan had seen going in and out of the buildings owned by the Board of Alkemists.

'Where did you learn to do this? Johnathan asked, awed at Jasmine's mother's abilities.

She smirked. 'I used to be part of a travelling theatre group. It was my job to make people look completely different to who they really were. I enjoyed it – almost as much as the pickpocketing we did while taking turns to be part of the audience. *Then* I had to go and fall for someone on the straight and narrow, who ended up working himself to death.'

'Father wasn't always so honest, Mother,' Jasmine said.

'True. We had great fun when we were younger. But then we had you and he got the silly idea that we should have you grow up as a well-rounded, honest and reliable young woman. As if that ever got anyone anywhere.'

CHAPTER 6

*E*rin led them through the front doors of the research facility's main reception, walking briskly with her pen poised in front of her clipboard (several of which they'd procured from a friend of Jasmine's mother, along with name badges to adorn the breast pockets of their lab coats, which had certainly done their job of convincing the guards outside that they were on official business).

After much discussion, Winkit had decided that it was best for her to go with them, but as it would have been highly unusual for inspectors to arrive with a cat in tow, she would have to hide. As a result, Johnathan was sporting a rounded stomach and Winkit was lamenting how sweat-ridden her fur had become because of his body heat.

With a brisk 'good afternoon', Erin handed the receptionist the letter she'd so carefully typed up and signed. As the receptionist processed what she was reading, Erin tapped her foot impatiently. Once understanding dawned, the receptionist jumped up, muttered an apology for keeping them waiting, and tugged twice on a bell-pull at the back of the room.

After a moment's delay, a short, stout man in a dark suit rushed in. Erin's eyebrow shot up as she recognised the head research manager, Mr Murston, but Jasmine nudged her in the ribs, and she regained control of her expression. 'I do hope this is a matter of some urgency, Mavis,' he said to the receptionist.

'Oh, it is, sir,' Mavis said and passed him the letter.

The effect it had on him was so transformative that Johnathan could hardly believe it was the same person. He turned to them, rather nervously. 'Ah, inspectors, you must forgive me for not greeting you right away, as you can imagine this is, uh, rather a surprise. Of course, I will grant you access to any area you require, as the director specifies. But may I ask, would you like a full tour of the facility first? I don't believe I've had the honour of showing you around before, so I must assume that you are new to the director's employ. It really is quite a maze in here, so it would be no trouble if you did need assistance in navigating. Perhaps I could show you the more exciting aspects of our work?'

'Thank you for the kind offer, Mr ...' Erin pretended to flick through the papers on her clipboard to find his name. 'Ah, yes, Murston. But we find we work best if we examine the facility with our own eyes from the start. You never know what tiny details might be missed otherwise.'

'Ah,' Mr Murston smiled weakly, 'indeed, indeed. Please, be our guests.' He gestured to the solid metal door to their left and produced a set of keys from his pocket to undo the tangle of locks keeping the door shut. The door opened with a teeth-jarring grind and they stepped through into a room lit with only the very dimmest of Kerical lights. 'We call this room the foyer. If you need my assistance, come back here and pull the green bell-pull beside you. You can increase the brightness in this room by clapping your hands, but please do not tamper with the light in any other room, for it could have a disastrous effect on some of our projects here.'

With that, he disappeared back through the door into the reception room, restoring the locks behind him. The moment he was out of sight, Winkit wriggled out from under Johnathan's shirt and jumped to the floor. 'Finally! It was hard to breathe in there, what with those clothes emanating such a strong scent of sickly fruit,' she said, smoothing her fur. She narrowed her green eyes, noticing how dark it was. 'Can you humans even see in here?'

'Not well,' Johnathan admitted. 'Did you hear what Mr Murston said about the lights? Clapping them increases the brightness. How is that possible?'

'It's one of the Kerical advances they're working on, I heard Mother and Father discussing it sometime last year before I left. As far as I understood, it was something to do with having the Kerical energy respond to specific sound waves. Try it,' Erin instructed.

Johnathan spread his hands apart and brought them together in a single, sharp clap. The lights flickered and went up a notch in brightness. Convinced, he clapped twice more until the lights were at an acceptable level for them to see by.

One wall was covered in nothing but coat hooks, most of them occupied by heavy windproof coats and a hat or two here and there. Then there was a small clock-in machine for the researchers to prove they'd been in, and beside it were four sets of locker cabinets, each set with fifteen individual lockers. Names had been assigned to each one in alphabetical order and after scanning all the ones under 'E', they finally came to Edwards, Renaldo. It was unlocked, bare inside except for the key belonging to it.

Everyone turned suspiciously to Erin. 'Are you absolutely sure that Mr Edwards would still have records here?' Johnathan asked.

'Yes, but they won't be in this room. And the only thing in those lockers is everyone's lunches anyway. It's not safe enough for anything else. Only the individual research floors offer any real security. Now, I'm having to go by memory on this, but I'm sure the floor Mr Edwards worked on was number seventeen, and this is floor zero. We need to head down to get to it.' She walked towards two identical doors on the far wall. Like the door they'd just come through, they were both made of metal, but thankfully there were no locks.

'Which one do we take?' Chester asked, noticing the distinct lack of signs.

'The one on the left-hand side. The other goes up, and it's just management offices up there, I think,' Erin replied, pulling at the door's great handle. The door was so heavy that it took both her and Chester's strength to inch it open enough for them all to slip through. The moment they released it, it swung shut behind them.

As they went down the steps, thankfully lit by adequate lamps along the walls, Johnathan fell into step with Erin. 'Do you really remember the way around this place from when you came here as a child?'

For the first time, he saw her laugh. 'No, Johnathan, though I wish my memory was as good as that. I know where to go because I happened across the building plans some weeks ago while looking for the tuning forks to go with Chester's violin and Jasmine's viola. They were just lying around in the family vault, so I took them along with a few other choice objects, like that necklace Jasmine gave to her mother.'

'Wait a moment, I thought you said—'

'That I didn't have much contact with my family? It's true, I don't. But I still sneak into the house every so often when supplies for the children are running low. That's how I got the idea for the Musical Bandits. The first night I snuck in, not long after I'd left, I was looking around the vault for something valuable to trade with the pawnbroker for enough Ren to buy food, but I saw four instrument cases tucked away under an old carpet roll. When I saw the violin, I immediately thought of Chester, who was employed by my father in our stables. He used to tell me about the music recitals he took part in before his parents died. When I spoke to him about the instruments one night a few months later, he told me that Samuel used to play the flute, and that neither of them particularly liked my parents as their employers.'

'Don't forget that I told you ages ago that I played the viola,' Jasmine cut in. 'I used to be Erin's maid – my father's idea before he died,' she added to Johnathan. 'They fired me when they found out we'd become friends, so I went back to work at the launderette with my mother.'

'Another reason why I decided to leave,' Erin said sourly. 'Anyway, eventually I told the three of them about the abandoned house I'd found and ended up living in, and the orphans that I'd taken in off the streets. They all decided to come and help me, as long as we found a means to survive ... and as my thanks, I gave them the instruments, taking the bodhran for myself so we could play together. Of course, when we gave a small performance in front of the children and they all fell asleep, we realised that they weren't ordinary instruments.'

'That's what made us think of how easy it would be to use them to steal, so now that's what we do!' Samuel said brightly, rubbing his hands together. In his disguise, Johnathan thought he looked like some sort of greedy businessman.

'But only to keep the children well fed and warm,' Chester added hastily, almost dropping his clipboard as the stairs made a sharp turn and he knocked it against the handrail.

'That may be the case for you,' Jasmine stated, 'but I see nothing wrong in the thrill and adventure of taking things of value from upper-class idiots. It's not as though they need them, anyway. We put the money to far better use. Besides, it's their fault the kids we've taken in needed to be rescued in the first place. All that Ren, and not a thought for anyone else, even though they walk past people living on scraps and having to sleep on doorsteps every day.'

As they descended, they took note of the floor numbers every time they came to a door. They were at number sixteen now; one more flight and they'd be in the right place.

Winkit raced ahead of them, impatient to explore, and when they hauled open the door to floor seventeen, she darted through it so quickly that she was just a flash of black and ginger fur. Taking her lead, they emerged into a spacious white room with work stations and cubicles filling most of it, aside from the path that edged around the different sections. Everything from the walls to the tiled floor was white: the tables and chairs, apparatus for measuring out ingredients, microscopes, pipes and tubing.

'I don't think I've ever fully appreciated colour until now,' Chester murmured, watching groups of researchers scurry back and forth between desks, weighing and measuring different objects and marking down the results.

Not one of them looked up as they passed, in fact, Johnathan was sure the researchers hadn't even noticed them come in. 'What are they all doing?' he whispered as the four of them pretended to take notes.

'I'm not sure. Their work is so obscure that most people can't even begin to guess, and I'm no exception to that. But Father's clearly got them working on *something*,' Erin whispered back.

Winkit appeared in front of them, her fur so bold against the stark whiteness that she stuck out like a firecracker. 'I found Renaldo Edwards' cubicle. Follow me,' she instructed and danced around a corner.

They followed her as quickly as they could while still trying to keep up their guise, but once they reached the desk where she was waiting, they found there was no need. Most of the cubicles on that side of the room were empty and those that weren't contained occupants so engrossed in their work that they wouldn't have heard a fire alarm if it were to go off.

Mr Edwards' desk was covered with files and loose scraps of paper, with a white typewriter at its centre. A dried-up inkwell stood beside it with a dozen broken pens, as well as a stained coffee cup that had been there so long that when Jasmine tried to move it, it stuck to the surface.

'I can't believe all his papers are still here,' Johnathan said, awed. 'It's been a month; why haven't they filed them away by now?'

'Who knows?' Samuel replied, picking up a handful of sketches depicting a timepiece with six hands and flicking through them.

'These look like just his initial findings ... any write-ups he might have done would have been handed straight to this level's supervisor and, as far as they're concerned, these are scraps of no interest,' Erin said, picking up each of the folders in turn, scanning their contents, and dropping them again. 'Unfortunately, it looks like this is of no use to us, either. Whatever he was doing with the Super Notes wasn't part of his normal research work.' She turned to Johnathan. 'You lived opposite him. Did you ever go into his apartment aside from the day he died?'

'Only once or twice.'

'And?' she pressed. 'Is there anything you recall about it that might help us? A certain way he piled his books or put away his shoes, even something unusual about the layout?'

Johnathan shook his head. 'No, the only thing I can tell you is that he was always very neat and tidy.' Then a memory stirred in his mind. 'There was one time when we caught each other on the stairs and stepped on the same loose step. I said that we should mention it to Mrs Higgins so that she could get someone in to repair it, but he said that you never know when a loose board might come in handy. He seemed such an honest man that I thought it was an unusual thing to say.'

Erin's brow creased and she muttered to herself, 'I wonder ... would he really have done something like that?'

'Don't tell me you think his work is buried under a loose step in Johnathan's apartment building?' Samuel asked, his voice pained. 'Do we have to go back there *again*?'

'No, I doubt he would have used somewhere *that* obvious. But that doesn't mean he didn't find, or make, a similar place to hide it here.' She looked meaningfully at the floor tiles, and suddenly they all caught on. 'Tap each one and try and find one that sounds hollow underneath or doesn't quite fit with the rest.'

Being as quiet as possible, they got down on their hands and knees and began checking each tile within Mr Edwards' cubicle space. Just as they were about to give up, Samuel found a slight chip in one under a small waste paper basket. He tapped it lightly; it shifted under his touch. 'It's this one,' he whispered. 'Jasmine, do you still have that pocketknife stashed away in your vest?'

'Here.' Without a shred of embarrassment, Jasmine pulled a folded knife from beneath her blouse. 'Oh, don't look at me like that,' she said as Johnathan and Chester stared at her. 'It's a useful thing to have, and keeping it there is simply convenient.'

Samuel took it, carefully prizing it into the slight gap on one side of the tile. With a flick of his wrist, he eased the tile up and put it to one side. In the gap beneath, he found a cloth-bound folder so full of papers and newspaper clippings that it had been tied shut with a piece of string. 'Does this look more like it?' He held it up to Erin.

A bang shook the whole room and, as they peered around the corner of the cubicle, they heard someone barking orders. Loud footsteps ensued, and there were several startled cries from the researchers still trying to carry on with their work.

'I'm not so sure I like the sound of this,' Johnathan said, turning to the others.

'You shouldn't,' Erin frowned. 'The man who's shouting is my father. We need to get out of here, *now!*'

'How? There's only one door leading out from the whole floor, and I'm pretty sure it's in use right now,' Chester said.

But Erin had taken a que from Jasmine and was already stuffing Mr Edwards' folder down her blouse and crawling along to the next few cubicles. At that moment, six guards with sizable batons came into view. They saw her immediately and rushed forwards.

here was a mad tangle of arms and legs as the guards made to capture the remaining Bandits and Johnathan. Having been caught first, Erin could only stand and watch. At least she still had the folder tucked away safely, the bulge it made hidden from view by her white lab coat.

Samuel tried to headbutt a guard in the stomach, but the guard was faster than him. With a precise block and sharp blow to his head using a baton, Samuel fell limply to the floor. The others gave up resisting at that point, letting themselves be hand-cuffed and led roughly back to the stairwell.

A gigantic figure stood in wait for them beyond the door; he possessed neatly cropped auburn hair the same shade as Erin's, gold-framed spectacles, and an air of extreme power and dominance. He studied them all with something between interest and con-tempt, judging by the mix of expressions crashing over his face.

'Take them to the holding cells on level zero-sev-en,' he hissed to the guards. 'And someone fetch Kingston. Quickly!'

The guards didn't hesitate, marching everyone back up the stairs and into the foyer, through the door leading up, and out onto the level marked zero-seven. The whole level was a prison. Cells in neat blocks were everywhere they looked, with the space between them creating a narrow walkway for the guards so that they could check on each individual occupant, and there were dozens. What was most surprising, however, was that the prisoners appeared to be researchers from other levels, judging from their clothing.

As they were taken to a block of vacant cells, they passed close by the researchers and heard them muttering, using short quick sentences often accompanied by gestures as though they were explaining something to a colleague, despite the fact that there was no one there to listen. Others had taken to hitting their heads against the bars, to the extent that they were bruised and bleeding.

The guards didn't stop them. In fact, if Johnathan had to make a guess, he would say the guards were actually enjoying the sight, for every time a researcher hit their head too hard and blacked out, the guards would snigger and make jibes. He even saw an exchange of coins as though they'd been betting on who would pass out first. It sickened him.

They came to a cell marked with the numbers seven-four-seven on a metal nameplate that had been welded to the top of the framework. The door was open and, in one synchronised movement, the guards holding them threw them inside, sliding the great steel door shut and bolting it so that it would be impossible to open from the inside. Then the guards walked away without sparing a second glance, leaving them to listen to the animated mutterings and rhythmic head banging of the imprisoned researchers.

Samuel, who had started to stir, was laid out on the single bench by Chester and Johnathan. He had a bump forming where he'd been hit, but at least his head wasn't bleeding or fractured.

'So, what do we do now?' Johnathan asked worriedly, looking back at them all. Despite their struggles, he saw that their disguises were fully intact. Fat lot of good now though, he thought dully. Erin's father had already seen through them, and the moment the man he'd sent for came to scrub their faces clean, their true identities would be on show for him to scrutinise. What would he think when he realised Erin was one of them?

Would he let her go to avoid any shame, or would he keep her there and humiliate her?

'He'll treat me exactly the same way as he'll treat you,' she said, reading his expression. 'My father's indifferent to me now. I dishonoured him by refusing to marry the man he'd chosen for me, so he doesn't even think of me as his daughter anymore. And as for what we're going to do now, we do the only thing we can. We wait.'

'Wait for what?' he asked.

'For him to interrogate us ... or for Winkit to return, whichever happens first.'

Johnathan blinked. Now that she mentioned it, he hadn't seen the cat since before they were captured.

Winkit had hidden behind a white waste paper bin while the guards hauled the Bandits and Johnathan away. The moment they had turned the corner to head back to the door, she ran around the other way, knowing from her explorations that the path between the cubicles was a perfect square, looping back round to the entrance.

If she was quick enough, she would beat the guards there.

The researchers, now that the sudden commotion on their level had subsided, had continued on with their work, paying attention to nothing else. They milled about, causing her to dodge between their clumsy feet, narrowly avoiding having her tail stepped on.

She reached the door just as she heard the guards coming around the opposite corner, but she put on an extra spurt of speed and slipped through the slight gap where a large, leather-shoed foot held it open. She'd hoped that whoever was behind there wouldn't be paying attention to anything but the approaching guards and their freshly caught prisoners. Unfortunately, she was wrong. No sooner was she through the door than a thick, frying-pan sized hand grasped her by the scuff of the neck and held her up.

'Now, what is a kitty such as yourself doing in a place like this?' the man asked, smiling wickedly. He reached for her collar to read the nametag, but instinct took over and Winkit tore at him with a flurry of teeth and claws. Deep scratches appeared on his arm and hand, but it was only when she bit into a nasty-looking scar on his thumb did he drop her in surprise.

Before he could grab her again, she charged up the stairs and waited by the door leading into the foyer for someone to come through. She didn't have to wait very long; a researcher with his face hidden behind an armful of glass jars full of coloured powders shouldered it open, straining visibly against the weight.

Darting through his legs, she went into the foyer, just as the heavy main door was being pushed closed by someone on the other side. By the time she reached it, the gap through was so small that she had to suck in her stomach to pass through, wishing that Molly hadn't fed her so many treats.

With relief she broke into the reception area, jumping onto the receptionist's desk, making her flinch and drop her coffee cup, then headed out the window, propped open enough to let in a waft of fresh air.

Outside once more, the temptation to freely roam the streets and inhale the sweet evening breeze was strong. She didn't even mind the cold slushy snow wetting her paws, such was her relief to get out of that place. Yet she knew she couldn't linger for long. She had to get to the meeting point and make the calling, a solemn cry for help to be heard only by other familiars.

A doddering old man with thick grey sideburns and a ragged beard hobbled into the prison room accompanied by a guard and headed straight for the cell where the Bandits and Johnathan were being kept. With him he carried a case so full that its contents – bottles of liquid and washcloths – could clearly be seen spilling from the top. He hummed softly to himself as he walked.

'Well, well, well,' he said when he saw them sitting resigned on the cell floor, leaning against the bars.

Samuel hadn't fully recovered, so his place was still on the bench, but his eyes focused on the old man with apprehension. 'When Director Stronghold sent for me, I wasn't told that there were five of you. This may prove to be my most interesting job for weeks.'

'Mr Kingston, I presume,' Erin said, standing up to assess him.

'Ah, so you've heard of me,' he said, impressed.

'No, we overheard you being summoned. But from the bottles filled with Easin Oil and Cole solution in your case, as well as the sheer quantity of washcloths, I can guess that you're here to remove our disguises.'

'Ah, a smart one, I see. How refreshing.'

The guard with him beckoned to another patrolling the area, requesting for the cell to be opened. 'I have the relevant clearance, as you well know,' Kingston told the cell guard, flashing a silver badge in front of the man's eyes. The cell guard exchanged a glance with his colleague and produced a set of keys from his belt, unlocking the door and sliding it open long enough for the old man to pass through.

Then, looking rather bored, the cell guard locked it back up and strolled off to continue his patrol while Kingston's guard, having performed his duty of fetching the old man, left the room.

'A rather unintelligent lot, the guards here,' Kingston grimaced, motioning for Samuel to get off the bench so that he could use it to set up a makeshift workstation. He unpacked his case, taking out the bottles and standing them side by side, along with tweezers, a blunt scraping tool resembling a butter knife and several other instruments that they didn't recognise. 'Now, I hope you won't cause me any trouble while I'm working; my heart's not as strong as it once was and I'd hate for you to be responsible for setting it off into a spasm. Who knows what they'd do to you then?' He spoke mildly but the threat he made was clear. 'Now you, girl, sit on the bench,' he called to Erin.

She did so without quarrel and he began dabbing her face with a cloth soaked in the oil she had recognised.

～

The alley smelled horrendous. Rubbish bins overflowed with rotten food, empty wrappers, and filthy rags. Some of the bins had been knocked over, their contents spilling out onto the snow like an outbreak of black mould.

Winkit wrinkled her nose as she trotted past, making her way to the carcass of a rusted motor carriage long stripped of its essential parts by thieves and ne'er-do-wells. Leaping up on what remained of its bonnet, she sat erect and let out a long high-pitched yowl. It echoed along the alley, making the rubbish bins resonate. She repeated it three more times, took a pause, and then started the call again.

Within minutes another cat appeared, a shorthaired tabby with a chunk missing from his tail. He sat in front of her and joined in her call. Another cat appeared, this time a fluffy white house cat, and did the same.

More and more cats arrived, each taking up the call with her until, at last, over a hundred familiars were present, filling the alley completely. 'My fellow familiars,' Winkit addressed them, raising her voice. 'I called you here tonight because there are a group of humans who need our help.'

An ancient Nodnol shorthair sniggered. 'When are there *not* humans who need our help?' she asked snidely. A few familiars sitting around her laughed.

Winkit cleared her throat, making them hush once more. 'I know it is unusual for a familiar whose Wytch has passed on to ask for help, but I'm sure you have all noticed that something in Nodnol is not right. The humans I wish to help are on the verge of discovering what this something is but, without our aid, they will be imprisoned indefinitely and by the time they are released, I fear it will be too late. My brothers and sisters, will you help me?'

There was a long pause, but then a white tortoiseshell broke the silence. 'You were once Irene Aqua's familiar, were you not?' she queried, noting Winkit's dual-coloured fur.

'That is correct,' Winkit replied, a small note of pride in her voice.

'Then I shall follow you,' the tortoiseshell declared. 'My mistress owed Irene a great debt, as I'm sure the Wytches of nearly every familiar here do. By helping you, I will in part be honouring that debt.'

There was a wave of agreement from around her and as she let out the call of acceptance, a single yowl that lasted for half a minute, the others joined her. Winkit was overwhelmed by their response and for a moment she felt the urge to mewl like a lost kitten having been reunited with its parents.

Blinking the tears away, she cleared her throat. 'Thank you, my friends. Now, the humans I wish to

rescue are being held on the upper floors of the
Board of Alkemists' research facility. There are no
windows that we can sneak through, aside from the
single one in the reception room, and the door
leading into the facility proper is covered with a series of locks and won't open unless all of them are unlocked in sequence, going from bottom to top. The
keys are being held by a man known as Mr Murston,
who I believe is still at the facility. As you all should
know, the Board of Alkemists makes every effort to
make sure all locks in the buildings they own are
Wytch-proof, so it will be no use to simply ask one of
your mistresses to stroll in there and undo them for
us. If a Wytch were even to try using her powers on
those locks, then their Alkemical traps would activate
and solidify her feet to the floor – or worse, if the rumours I've heard are anywhere near true. There are
no air vents leading from the reception room to the
other side of the door either, so there truly is only a
single way through.'

'This is a tricky one to be sure,' the tortoiseshell
commented. 'Does this Mr Murston carry the keys on
his person, or does he leave them somewhere?'

'I believe he carries them on him,' Winkit replied,
knowing how impossible the rescue was beginning to
sound.

'He has a spare set, I think.'

Winkit stared as a grey kitten walked forwards,
barely old enough to be allowed to respond to the call.
'My mistress saw them hanging up in a safe once in
Mr Murston's home study. She works there as a maid.
I'm sure she could figure out the combination to the
lock,' the kitten continued, his voice barely a squeak.

'But your mistress can only be a child, if your age

is anything to go by,' the tabby who'd first appeared said. 'Is she even in control of her powers yet?'

'Of course she is,' the kitten said defensively, flicking his tail.

'Calm yourself, young one,' the tortoiseshell chided him. 'Now is not the time for arguments. Tell us what you have seen your mistress do so far, and we shall access her ability.'

'She can make plants grow from seeds in a few seconds, create a flame in her palm, levitate things, *and* she can even fly on her broom ... only on nights when it's foggy though,' he added hastily at the number of concerned looks he received.

'Be that as it may, those skills are very different to the one needed to detect the right combination for a safe. What are her puzzle-solving skills like? Is she good at riddles and strategy games?' Winkit pressed.

'Yes, she beats all her friends at chess every time, and has worked through every riddle posed to her by her aunt, the Wytch Clarice,' the kitten answered.

Winkit scratched behind her ear. 'Is Wytch Clarice's familiar here?' she called, searching the sea of fur and whiskers before her for a response.

A black cat with white socks stepped forwards and sat beside the kitten. 'I am Wytch Clarice's familiar. I can attest to what young Poppets here claims. His mistress, the young Wytch Frances, is indeed talented for her age. She should have no problem getting into the safe and taking the keys, even without using her magic if need be, though I suspect this Mr Murston wouldn't have bothered to make his own locks Wytch-proof. He has no idea the one dusting his shelves and helping to prepare supper every day is a Wytch,' he said proudly, giving Poppets a fond lick.

Poppets pulled a face, but couldn't help straightening up importantly, forgetting that he was several inches shorter than every other familiar there.

Winkit's whiskers twitched in amusement. 'Very well, then,' she said. 'Our first plan of action is to enlist the young Wytch Frances to our cause. Let the rescue begin!'

CHAPTER 8

'There, don't you all feel better now that you're not hiding your true selves anymore?' Kingston asked, methodically putting all the jars and washcloths neatly back into his case, being careful to keep the used ones from the single clean cloth that was left. The amount of make-up Jasmine's mother had covered them in had truly astonished him. He had expected a lot to come off Erin and Jasmine's faces, for he knew that it wasn't uncommon for teenage girls to dress themselves up with the stuff so that they could go to balls and other functions which only adults were allowed to attend; he'd thus assumed they would be a lot younger than they first appeared, but the boys had even more caked on their faces.

The boys' beards and moustaches had obviously been fake, he had been able to tell that from a quick glance. All of it had been made from dyed goat fur, specially treated to remove the tell-tale barnyard smell that most people associated with common goat-fur products. But the age spots and wrinkles around the eyes and brows, as well as the slightly thickened eyebrows, that was a difficult effect to achieve.

Though they refused to speak about it, he was sure a master artist had assisted them with their disguises, and he would certainly be reporting as much to Director Stronghold upon his return to the offices two levels down.

'I say, whatever the reason for this charade, you must be aware that the consequences are rather more serious than most other crimes in Nodnol. I hope your cause is worth it,' he said sternly, signalling to a passing guard that he was finished.

'Oh, believe us when we say it is,' Samuel said darkly, nursing the newly risen bump on his head.

Kingston shrugged and, as the guard opened the cell door to let him out, chuckled quietly to himself. 'Foolish children, sneaking into a facility with such hazardous objects lurking about. It was a miracle that none of them stumbled into one of the testing rooms for new technologies. Risky, even for the Alkemists who work here,' he muttered, just loud enough for them to hear.

He didn't see Samuel make a rude gesture at his back.

❧

'Come on, Poppets, you know I can't do any magic while I'm working. Even if I had the time, what if someone were to see me?' Frances asked, dusting the windowsill where Poppets was perched on the outside.

It was nearly five and preparations for dinner were being made. Cook would be calling her soon to help prepare the sweet dish, and then the table had to be laid.

'This is more important,' Poppets insisted. 'I've got every Wytch's familiar counting on me to convince you. I already had to argue to make them believe you're strong enough to do it.'

'Well, that's your problem, not mine,' Frances said harshly and turned away to carry on with her other chores.

There was a creaking of hinges and a soft thud as four paws landed on the ground. Frances sighed. 'What have I told you about coming in the house while it's still daytime, Poppets?' she began, turning back around. But instead of Poppets, who was still outside looking through the window, there was another cat looking at her. She stared at it, taking in its dual-coloured fur: half black, half ginger.

By the way it seemed to be assessing her, from the frizzy strands of brown hair hanging down from her maid's bonnet to the stains around her knees where she'd recently been scrubbing the floor, it was clearly more than just a pet cat. *Another Wytch's familiar, then.* It even twitched its whiskers the same way Poppets did when he gave an approximation of a smile.

'Forgive me for imposing on you, Frances,' Winkit said, keeping her voice hushed as another servant rushed past the door, oblivious to what was going on in the room. 'But Poppets is telling the truth. We really do need your help to rescue a group of humans.'

Frances frowned. 'Even if that's true, why should I risk losing my one source of income to help you? Just whose familiar are you?'

'The very fact that you've asked that question proves to me that you are no fool. Indeed, you remind me very much of my mistress when she was young. Her name was Irene ... perhaps you've heard of her?'

'Irene? I'm sure I don't know any Wytches with that name. None that are still alive, any –wait, did you say "was"? Your mistress *isn't* alive anymore, is she? Then ...' Frances' eyes grew wide. 'Are you really the familiar of *Irene Aqua?*'

Winkit purred.

'But she's, well, pretty much the stuff of legend among my generation. The things she did ... she was so brave, and so powerful.'

'Yes, the things she did were brave, even revolutionary in some ways, if you consider that Wytches all used to work independently without trusting one another. But she was an ordinary woman doing what she believed in,' Winkit chuckled. 'She hated the idea of anyone putting her on a pedestal. Besides, her curiosity was the very reason the Alkemists set to developing Wytch-proof locks. Not that they *knew* it was her sneaking into the safes of all the rich households. In fact, if people hadn't started to realise that there were less homeless on Nodnol's streets, I doubt those families would even have noticed what she took from them.'

She curled her tail around herself, licking the fur on her chest nonchalantly. 'You know, the humans we need to help have a similar mindset to hers. They rescue orphaned children off the streets and take care of them. I'd hate to think what would happen to those children if their guardians never return home.'

Frances bit her lip. 'I suppose if there's no chance of them escaping otherwise, and if Mr Murston doesn't find out about me ... alright, I'll help you. What do you need me to do, exactly?'

'The only way to free them is by taking the keys that Mr Murston has in his safe. Poppets has told us you have the ability to open such a safe. Is he telling the truth?'

'Yes, I ... I think so. One of the key tactics for working out the combination to a safe is to know the person who it belongs to, and have an understanding of how they think. I've worked for Mr Murston since I was eight; he's a strict man but a fair one, and unless he's stressed, quite logical. As long as I can figure out the first digit, I can easily use my powers to encourage the rest of the mechanism into turning to the right code. I know his ones aren't Wytch-proof; those things feel like I've stepped into a cold shower when I'm near them.' She paused momentarily, putting her hands on her hips. 'Still, this whole idea is ludicrous. I can't just sneak in there and fiddle about with his things. It won't be long until he comes home anyway, maybe an hour at the most, and Wytch-lore help us if dinner's not ready by then.'

'I don't believe you have to worry about Mr Murston arriving home at his usual time. I have it on the best authority that he'll be somewhat delayed tonight. Something happened at the research facility that he ... did not expect,' Winkit said mysteriously.

Frances eyed her doubtfully. 'These people you want to rescue, they didn't do anything *illegal*, did they? It's all just a misunderstanding; they were in the wrong place at the wrong time, right?'

'Sometimes the line between legal and illegal must be stretched when searching for information that could help prevent others from a terrible fate, wouldn't you agree?' Winkit replied, deliberately vague.

'I suppose so,' Frances said. 'So ... how can we keep Cook and everyone else from wondering where I am? I'm never late helping with dinner preparations; it'll be awfully suspicious if I'm not there.'

Winkit swished her tail knowingly. 'Tell me, Frances, have you ever had any rats in the kitchen? Or mice?'

'Once or twice, but Cook's always managed to chase them out with a broom.'

'Are you sure there aren't a few left, hiding in the pantry, or under the workbench?' she pressed. 'I have a few friends with me this evening, and we could all use some exercise to warm our paws from this dreadful snow.'

Frances grinned, catching on. 'It's not *impossible* that we've overlooked a few.'

~

Screams from the kitchen as a hundred cats leapt through the windows and into the pantry, bombarding Cook and servants alike, carried up to Mr Murston's study where Frances, Winkit and Poppets quietly slipped through the door.

It wasn't locked. Why should it be? Mr Murston never suspected that he had a Wytch for a maid, or that any of his servants would be bold enough to try tackling the combination lock on his safe.

'Okay,' Frances said, turning on one of the Kerical lamps by the desk. The safe was located on the wall opposite, hidden by a gold-framed portrait of Mr Murston and his wife, who was thankfully holidaying with her sister in the countryside. Frances shuddered at the thought of confronting *her* in this situation. Even in the portrait, her severity carried through. She had a stare that was well-known for sending the other maids and Cook fleeing from her presence. Frances had only come under it once, an experience she never wished to repeat.

She pulled the portrait forwards, letting it swing on the hidden hinges attached to one side. The combination lock was a heavy black thing, matching the metal of the safe itself. It was a complicated one, for not only were there numbers, but letters as well, and the combination was a nine-digit code. There was also a phial of clear liquid attached to the dials. She tilted the lock sideways, making the liquid move from side to side. It was slow, unlike water, as though it was slightly sticky.

'Uh-oh. We might have a problem. This lock is more complicated than I thought. There are so many different combination possibilities that it will take more than my magic to open it, even if I do guess the first digit. And there's a trap mechanism too; if the wrong code is put in, I have a feeling it will seal the lock solid. But I suppose we can still try for clues to find the whole code. It'll be a word and number combination, I'm sure of it, so we can look for a word that might have a number by it, or even a date,' she explained.

'It's a slim chance, but if it truly does have a trap mechanism as you say, then searching is a far better option than you trying your magic and accidentally locking us out entirely,' Winkit agreed.

There were three stained oak bookcases next to the desk and a writing bureau in front of the oval window, the wood long since faded by the sun. Frances decided to look in there first while Poppets and Winkit looked through the assortment of books, pulling them out one by one and shaking them to see if any papers came loose, then examining the inside covers for scribbled notations.

Opening the bureau's front, Frances found it full of tiny compartments filled with notepapers, pens and inkwells. There was even a small perfume bottle, and when she picked up a thick envelope containing fine writing paper of the kind usually used for official documents, she found that it carried the same scent as the bottle. 'This is odd,' she said, more to herself than the cats. 'This bureau has been in here for years, but never did I think anyone but Mr Murston used it.'

She held up the perfume bottle and the scented papers for them to see.

'Does his wife not come in here?' Winkit asked, but Poppets laughed beside her.

'I haven't seen Mrs Murston much, nor been close to her apart from the time she caught me by the rubbish bins and tried to kick me while shrieking about fleas, but I can tell you that when she's home, she's never around Mr Murston unless they're at the dining table, and even then, they sit at opposite ends,' the kitten smirked.

'What about a daughter?' Winkit said.

Frances shook her head. 'The Murstons don't have any children. There was a niece, though,' she said, suddenly remembering. 'She was a shy girl, and away at boarding school most of the time. She did love visiting here, though. Maybe Mr Murston let her write in here. I was only young at the time and not allowed to clean the upper rooms, so I can't be sure.'

'Why do you speak of this girl in past tense?' Winkit questioned.

'She died. Two years ago, I think. Her parents had an early version of those motor carriages that are so popular now, but it had a faulty connection. They crashed; her parents died from the impact, and she a few days later in hospital. The Murstons were devastated. They were the ones who had gifted them the motor carriage.'

Winkit narrowed her eyes and leapt elegantly onto the bureau, investigating for herself. At the back of the compartment, where the perfume had been, was a silver catch. Reaching in with her paw, she flicked the catch up. With a click, a secret compartment shot out from the front of the bureau. In it was a bejewelled diary, and underneath were the blueprints for a motor carriage. In the corner of the blueprints, in scribbled writing, were the words: Prototype number eleven.

'I think we've found the number,' Winkit said. 'Now we just need the word. Is there anything in the diary?'

'If the number is only two digits and the total needs to be nine ... it would be seven letters, wouldn't it?' Frances thought aloud. She opened the diary to the first page. In the same handwriting as on the blueprints, was a message. *To my dearest niece Aiyanna, on your eighteenth birthday. I give you this diary to record all your wonderful ideas on auto Alkemy and to inspire you, I have enclosed the blueprints to the motor carriage I am to gift to your father next week. Much love, Uncle Frederick.*

'This is it. Here, her name: Aiyanna. Seven letters!' Frances exclaimed. She ran over to the safe, about to put in the code, but then stopped short. 'Which way around should I put them? We've only got one try!'

'Stay calm, Frances,' Winkit chided, while Poppets rubbed soothingly against Frances' legs. 'Let me think.' She took a look at the diary and blueprints once more. It struck her that Murston had placed them in the secret compartment in a certain way, diary on top and blueprints underneath. In the note, he had also praised Aiyanna on her ideas first and then mentioned the motor carriage. It wasn't much to go on, but it was the only clue they had. 'Try putting her name first, and then the numbers at the end,' she said at last.

Hesitantly, Frances followed her directions. There was a sharp click, and the combination lock popped open, allowing access to the safe. Realising that she'd been holding her breath, Frances inhaled deeply and opened the safe's door. As expected, hanging on a small hook was the collection of keys that Winkit so dearly needed. She took them down and put them on the floor by the familiar.

'Go and get your friends,' she advised with a smile.

'Will you be alright tidying up in here?' Winkit asked, examining the room. The bookshelves were a complete mess.

'I think so. And with all the commotion the other familiars are causing downstairs, even if Mr Murston does come home on time, he'll have his hands full trying to get an explanation from Cook. Though I expect you'll have to call them off now, won't you?'

'Indeed, I must. You'll be a great fully fledged Wytch one day, Frances,' she said.

'But I didn't use my magic at all like you'd hoped,' Frances pointed out.

'There's far more to being a Wytch than using

magic. Logic and observation are a fine thing too,' Winkit replied, picking the keys up with her mouth.

They went back down to the sitting room where Frances had been dusting, and both Winkit and Poppets jumped onto the windowsill. 'Don't wait up for me, Frances,' Poppets called behind him as he sprang out to land in a fresh clump of snow outside. 'Told you, didn't I?' he said to Winkit.

'It's impolite to brag,' she mumbled through a mouthful of keys and, dashing to the window by the kitchen, they made the call to signal to the other familiars that it was time to go.

One by one the cats exited the house, their tails flicking in delight. 'I haven't had that much fun in years,' the tortoiseshell said as she ran to meet them. 'Perhaps we should gather together more often.'

CHAPTER 9

'*E*rin, how good to see you,' Arthur Stronghold said as he peered at her through the bars. His hair was flecked with grey, yet even so, his age did nothing to lessen his authoritative manner. He scanned the others with an amused look on his face. 'What interesting friends you appear to have made, too.'

He took a notebook from behind his back and, as he opened it, they glimpsed black and white photographs alongside pages of neatly typed notes. 'I see we have dear Chester and his charming little brother, Samuel. I wondered where the two of you scurried off to so quickly. A terrible shame, particularly you, Chester; the horses always seemed much more content with you around. Perhaps they sensed you had a similar mindset to them, that herd mentality to want to follow along behind someone. I wonder what your poor departed parents would say if they could see you now. Would they be proud to know that their sons have turned into little sneaks, cheating your way in here under the guise of an inspector?' he asked acidly. He checked his notes.

'They had quite the inking business, didn't they? A pity that you would bring shame to such a good family name.'

He turned the page dramatically. 'Ah, Jasmine, the most slapdash maid I've ever had the pleasure of firing. Now I'm sure *your* mother knows *exactly* what you've been up to. Those suits and lab coats you're all wearing certainly appear professional. I wonder if the laundrette has misplaced any similar garments this week?'

Jasmine swept forward to speak, her face flushing with rage, but Chester grabbed her arm. They both knew it would do no good to argue with Erin's father, he was more than capable of using their words against them.

Next, he turned to Johnathan. 'Now then, the others I can understand, they're all a questionable sort anyway. You however, my lad, simply don't fit. According to my team of investigators, you were apprenticed under Alfred Vancold for three years as an Alkemical Apothecary, but upon the closure of his shop last month, have been working as ...' he scanned the page several times, shaking his head disapprovingly, 'a door-to-door *salesman* selling some enchanted gimmick. How very sad for you, with what would have been such a *promising* career, only to be reduced to this.'

He shut his notebook with a snap. 'I'm sure I don't need to say this, but you can certainly forget working at any other Alkemical Apothecaries to complete your training after this little stunt; I'll make sure of it.' He faced Erin. 'There now, how do you feel knowing that your studious friend has lost all chance of working in his chosen field because of tallying up with you? And the rest of you will be labelled as criminals for the remainder of your lives?'

'You're always so petty, Father, so smug to think that you can one-up whoever you want,' she spat at him, glaring.

'Petty? My dear daughter, you have me all wrong. I just take pleasure in dwelling upon the small details in life, however filthy and unscrupulous they may be,' he replied, flashing her a nasty grin. 'But now on to serious matters. Why did you feel it necessary to come in here? What were you after?'

'As if I'd tell you,' Erin said flatly. 'I'd rather sit here and rot.'

'Really? How fascinating. I must tell you though, these are the luxurious cells; they're usually only reserved for my poor employees over there.' He gestured to the muttering researchers. 'They have so little time to relax ... sometimes their minds simply unravel every now and then. I can arrange for you to stay at the prison, however. You might not know, as it's been freshly built, but I own a whole wing there now, dedicated to people who try to steal our work and leak it to the public. It's been happening rather a lot lately. It seems that someone is desperate to know what technology we're working on, going so far as to kidnap people.'

'Kidnap?' Erin asked, forgetting her anger. 'Who?'

'I thought you'd be able to tell me that yourself, but if you truly don't know, at least that rules out *one* of my suspicions about your activities. An Alkemical Sculptor, *the* Alkemical Sculptor actually. I've never seen work more stunning that his. His name is Richard Pines and for the last few years we've had him down on level eight, trying to perfect a safer, more durable casing for our latest line of motor carriages. He disappeared two months ago, and we haven't found a trace of him since.'

'What about employees that have died recently? Like Renaldo Edwards? Do you think it could be linked somehow?' Johnathan asked curiously. Despite his dislike of the man, he'd seen immediately that the longer they kept Arthur talking, the more likely the director was to spill other information.

Arthur blinked at him, as though he'd forgotten he and the others were there. 'Edwards? Edwards, Edwards ... ah, yes, I recall him now. Worked down on level seventeen and died at the beginning of the month. Yes, your records did say that you were his neighbour,' he said, stroking his chin. 'A shame to lose him, to be sure. He wasn't bad at his job, but that's the unfortunate thing about the human condition: people have a habit of dying without warning. In answer to your question, no, I don't think there's any connection there. As I say, Edwards was a decent researcher, yet he was nothing special, nor did he know anything of real substance. He was but a single ant in an enormous colony.'

The door to the level opened with a bang, and three guards rushed in along with Mr Murston. Arthur shot daggers at them with his eyes. 'What the blazes is going on now?' he roared, making them freeze in their tracks.

'We're sorry to disturb you, sir, but the entire building has been overrun by cats!' Murston announced, red in the face.

Arthur looked at him as though he'd lost his mind. 'Overrun by *what*?'

'Cats, sir,' one of the guards next to him said. 'I

don't know how many, but it looks like a hundred of them. They all came spilling in from nowhere. We don't have enough men to get rid of them all.'

'For goodness' sake, man. Use your brain. How many Alkemists do we have on shift this evening, Murston?' Arthur asked.

'About sixty, sir,' Murston replied, using his fingers to do a few calculations

'Then round them all up and get them to help you. It shouldn't be too difficult.'

'With respect, sir, you haven't seen just how many felines there are. And they're so *quick*. They've already caused substantial damage to the reception room and the foyer, and they were making their way towards the lower levels, too.'

'I don't believe this. Of all the incompetent ...!' He turned back to the cell, where Johnathan, Erin, Samuel, Chester and Jasmine were trying not to let the excitement they felt leak onto their faces.

There was only one reason for a hoard of cats to attack the facility – Winkit was trying to help them.

'It seems our meeting will have to be cut short. But believe me when I say that I'll find out what you're up to!' He strode away towards the door with Mr Murston and the guards falling into step behind him.

The guards normally patrolling the cells were summoned too, so for a while the Bandits and Johnathan were left with just the company of the insane researchers, still mumbling and milling around in their individual cells. But it wasn't for long, because a great explosion sounded several levels beneath them and seconds later the level door was opened again, not by the guards, but by a towering pyramid of cats, all balancing precariously on top of one another so they could reach the handle.

They had no time to be stunned by the sight. Winkit was suddenly upon them, thrusting a tangle of keys through the bars. 'One of them is a skeleton key for every cell,' she said, breathing heavily.

Most of the keys were brass or silver, but there were three made of steel like the cells. Trying them one by one, Erin found the one they needed and turned it. The cell unlocked easily, and once they were all out, the cats led them back over to the door. 'What was that explosion just then?' Jasmine asked as they came out onto the stairwell. It was filled with dense red smoke that smelled heavily of metal.

'No time to explain,' Winkit yowled. 'Head to the reception room. The foyer door should be open. I'll tell you everything back at the house!'

'Will you be alright?' Johnathan asked, concerned. 'How will you and all the others get out?'

'Never mind that, just go!' she yelled, and swiped him with her claws to make him run.

He did so, along with the others, and when then got to the foyer, the door into the reception room was indeed unlocked. In fact, it had been blown clean off its hinges along with most of the wall.

It was dark outside and bitterly cold as they made their way to the abandoned street where the Bandits had their burnt-out house. The wind made their lab coats billow behind them, and the snow was so icy and wet that it soaked them right up to the knees.

When they finally arrived, shivering and sneezing, the orphaned children huddled round them, demanding to know where they'd been. Johnathan hadn't expected there to be a dozen of them, he'd thought four or five at the most. Now he knew how convenient it had been for the Bandits to steal for their income; not even the four of them could earn enough to feed these many mouths three times a day, as well as wash and cloth them.

Lighting the Kerical lamps in the sitting room, Erin handed out cosy blankets to everyone and made mugs of hot chocolate to warm their hands. With Johnathan's help, she cooked up a light supper for the children and made sandwiches for the others, who were calming the children down and trying to come up with a satisfactory reason for why they hadn't been home on time.

Once they'd all eaten, they put the children to bed and finally settled down to rest. Except that they couldn't. A loud hammering sounded at the front door and before they could get up, Molly stormed into the house carrying a very singed Winkit in her arms.

'How dare you!' Molly shouted. 'What have you lot *done* to her?' She put Winkit gently on the floor and dragged one of the unused blankets from the open cupboard, folding it neatly so Winkit could lie on it. 'I was on my way here to check up on you and to see if she could come home, but instead I found her wandering about in the snow like this.'

Winkit looked up at them wearily. 'I'm sorry,' she said. 'I tried to explain what happened, but she wouldn't listen.' She eased herself down onto the blanket. 'Johnathan, I don't suppose you happen to have your ingredient bag with you?'

Johnathan shook his head. 'No, I left it back at my apartment. I didn't think we'd need it.'

'Actually, Johnathan, it's not there,' Jasmine said. 'Not all of it, anyway.' She put her hand inside her blouse again and, when she took it out, she held the packets containing his ingredients.

He raised an eyebrow.

'What? It was Erin's idea; she chose which ones to take. She said they might come in handy. I took them when you fainted,' she said, pulling out yet another handful.

'That wasn't what I was questioning. How do you hide all this down ... down there?' he asked, feeling a blush creep into his cheeks.

Jasmine laughed. 'All my vests have pockets sewn on the inside, and I've altered the cut of my clothes to accommodate them. It's a good hiding place, no-one ever thinks to check there.'

'Chester w—'

'Not *now*, Samuel,' Erin cut in. 'Winkit, tell me what you need, and Johnathan and I will mix it for you. Jasmine has most of the essentials, so I'm sure we can help.'

'A simple painkiller would work. I just need something to dull the ache in my muscles. That explosion and the few that came after it really quite battered me,' Winkit told her.

'Speaking of those explosions, what exactly caused them, and how did you get all those familiars to follow you? Heck, how did you even get back *in* the facility?' Chester asked as Erin and Johnathan searched through the ingredients to find the ones they needed.

As the medicine brewed for the next few minutes,

Winkit recounted everything that she'd done since they were captured, including having Frances get Mr Murston's spare keys. 'After that, it was easy. The reception was closed for the day, but the window was open enough to let us crawl through. We unlocked the security door and, using some of the acrobatics that you saw and sheer force of numbers, we got it open and rushed through to the foyer.

'We split into several groups to tackle as many floors as we could, causing enough damage to draw Stronghold's attention away from you and onto us. The first explosion was an accident, one of us knocked over a phial of liquid that landed in an open barrel of motor carriage fuel. Luckily, the familiars who set it off were quick enough to hide behind some new kind of casing stacked in the same room. Everything else went up in flames aside from that. Shortly after, I discovered where they were holding you from Stronghold's own mouth as he rushed to the lower levels. He was in such a fury that he didn't even suspect my group were hiding in the shadows on the stairwell.'

She paused while Johnathan placed the bowl of medicine in front of her. She took a few licks, shaking her whiskers in distaste, and then continued. 'I sent a scout down to tell the others that if they found anything flammable, to set it off if they could. I didn't think that anyone would try to *throw* anything flammable, or explosive, at us in return. That's why the door to the reception room was blown apart. As the majority of familiars made to escape while I was on my way to get you, one of the researchers chased them with a handful of ball bombs.'

'Ball bombs? What in Phlamel's name would they

have those for down there for?' Johnathan inquired, aghast. 'Were the familiars hurt?'

'Only a few singed tails; they all made it home in one piece,' Winkit said.

Erin tutted. 'Oh, come on, Johnathan. You must have realised by now that my father is using the research facility to develop some very questionable things. He's not a very nice man. Just look at how delighted he was to destroy your career ...' She looked away from him. 'For what it's worth, I'm sorry about that.'

Johnathan smiled at her. 'To be honest, I think it was over already. None of the other Alkemical Apothecaries I approached even wanted to talk to me. One of them even said my methods were "quaint" and "impractical". And given what I've seen today, I don't think I want to be credited for by ability by the Board of Alkemists. I'd rather do my own thing.'

Impulsively, Erin took his hand and squeezed it. 'You're an unusual boy, Johnathan Nesbit, but one I would be proud to call my friend.'

Behind them, Samuel pretended to vomit, but Jasmine twisted his ear.

'Fascinating as that is,' Molly said, making sure that Winkit had finished drinking her medicine, 'may I ask what you got from doing all this?'

'This,' Erin said smugly, producing Mr Edwards' folder from her blouse and adding to Johnathan, 'I have pockets in all of my vests, too.'

CHAPTER 10

*F*inishing their hot chocolate, the Bandits, Johnathan, and Molly (who had calmed down enough to accept a cup of chocolate of her own), huddled together on one of the less moth-eaten rugs to read the folder together. Their blankets were still wrapped tightly around and their toes remained cold, but they were too eager to find out what Mr Edwards had written to delay reading it any longer.

Carefully, Erin untied the string binding the folder together and opened up the front cover. She took out the handful of loose papers from the top and spread them across the floor so they could read them clearly. There were newspaper clippings, shipping reports, receipts, sketches, and three missing persons reports.

'Look at this,' Winkit said, pawing at one of the sketches. It was a set of scales with a black circle on one side and a white circle on the other, the very same symbol they'd found at the bottom of the box of Super Notes.

'So, he really was researching them,' Johnathan said with some relief. He scanned one of the shipping reports. It was from a delivery service in central Nod-nol, two streets away from the research facility. Thirty vials of stamping ink had been delivered to the back gates of the facility itself. The notes were very specific about the package being sent to the back gates rather than any others and had been typed in upper case for even more clarity. He showed Chester, indicating the sender's name. 'Have you heard of those Inkers?' he asked.

Chester examined the name. 'No, but that might only mean they set up business recently. The address they've given for their business is a home address, not a shop. I'd say it's a one-man operation, someone trying to build a client list before he sets up shop properly. It's not uncommon; having a shop is a big investment when there's so much competition around. What's curious, though, is that this house is right on the city's outskirts. I know for a fact that there are ten very respectable Inkers between there and the research facility. Why didn't the client choose one of them instead?'

'To try and keep their order from keen eyes, per-haps,' Erin suggested. 'If the inker is small and inde-pendent with few clients, he would be less inclined to talk about them for fear of losing them. Bigger Inkers can employ up to a hundred people, especially the ones used by commercial companies, and one or two of them might have loose tongues. If you wanted to keep something secret, wouldn't you avoid that too? Let's see what Renaldo wrote about it all.'

She flicked through the main contents of the folder, a stack of bound papers that appeared to be a journal. Dismissing most of the early entries because of their lack of relevance, she got halfway through and stopped. 'Here, listen to this. "June 4th. I visited a friend this afternoon who had recently been sent a flyer about a new product called Super Notes, calling for sellers who wanted to earn an extra few Ren. The claims on how easy they were to sell and just how much Ren one could expect to make from them sounded incredulous to me, but my friend had been taken in by it and ordered several boxes of the things straight away. Despite my insistence that this venture would most likely end in failure, he was excited at the prospect, and gave me a full rundown of the product specifications. My interest was piqued immediately, not because I suddenly felt the urge to purchase any, but because they sounded so very like objects enchanted by a Wytch. (I know for certain there is no Alkemy as yet developed that can make a piece of paper *sing*.)"'

'That *is* what we thought, too,' Johnathan pointed out, but Erin waved her hand.

'There's more. "June 14th,' she continued. '"My friend contacted me five days ago to say that the Super Notes he'd ordered had arrived, and would I like a sample or two to examine. I took him up on that offer and brought them back to my cubicle at the facility. Having finished my final reports on my other work, I took to studying these Super Notes immediately. I first tested each type of pad to see if they really did have the abilities that were advertised, and was immediately greeted with note papers floating around my head, while others let off sweet perfumes and sung my scribblings to me in sweet voices. Having established that they did perform, I then carried out several tests to find out if they truly were the work of a Wytch, for after the director ordered the interrogation of Irene Aqua some years ago, we now know that enchantments leave slight traces on the objects they're cast on, and that these traces can be detected by Alkemical means if the right solution is used. Yet all of these tests came back negative, so I have been forced to conclude that my initial assumption of how they work is false.

"'I did, however, accidentally catch the corner of one of these Super Notes with a match as I made to light my pipe. The most curious thing happened. Green smoke rose up from the singed paper, and I thought I heard a scream. Ludicrous as it sounds, it was almost as though I'd burnt a *person*, not simply paper. This was a most interesting thought, and eager to pursue it, I allowed the Super Notes to burn fully. To my horror, apparitions appeared over each of the smoking remains – apparitions of people. Though they were formed of smoke, there was a distinct moment of clarity when I could make out their features and saw that they were all women before they dispersed into the air. What troubles me most is that I do not think these apparitions were a simple illusion, an effect created to scare anyone who wishes to dispose of the Super Notes, but something far worse. I must get these away from my friend. I have no evidence other than a gut feeling, but these notepads are somehow dangerous.

"'June 17th. I arrived at my friend's house a little after noon. It is a Saturday, so I was sure he would be home, but after knocking at the door, I was met with no response. Fearing that he might have taken ill, I climbed through his kitchen window, only to find him collapsed on the floor. I immediately hailed a motor carriage taxi to send for a Doktor, but when the good man arrived, my friend had already taken his last breath. Unsure of the cause, the Doktor has endeavoured to provide a full autopsy, but in the meantime, I must continue my studies of the notepads. I have taken the boxes from his home and stored them at my own apartment. At least that way, any prospective buyers will be spared whatever ill effects they might have, for already I feel fatigued from my study of them, and I know that it is not simply a cause of the intensity of my work. Whatever the true purpose of these things may be, the general public must not get their hands on them!'"

Johnathan swallowed heavily as Erin finished the entry. It was exactly as he'd feared. Mr Edwards had wanted for him to keep the Super Notes hidden, but instead he'd sold them to some of the richest families in Nodnol, and now their lives were in danger because of the disease which had struck them all.

'Forget it, Johnathan.' It was Samuel, for once being serious. He and the others had been watching the play of expressions on Johnathan's face, and knew what he'd been thinking. 'No one could possibly have figured that out. You did what any normal person would do who was broke and suddenly found a means to earn Ren.'

'I never thought I'd say this, but my brother's right,' Chester added, rubbing Samuel's head. Samuel stuck out his tongue. 'What's done is done, and it was *not* your fault. Erin, are there more entries?'

'Yes, a lot,' she said, scanning ahead. 'He mentions that the autopsy of his friend revealed that he died from an extreme case of Acute Energy Loss, something that the Doktor had never seen before. It got to him in a matter of days. Renaldo also notes that his own fatigue was growing; the longer he concentrated his energies on testing the Super Notes, the more strained he became. None of his experiments to find out what the apparitions were came out successfully, but he had begun digging around for who was producing them near the end of August. Like us, he discovered the set of scales mark and looked it up in the compendium of Nodnol businesses. Again, he came back with nothing, but by chance, he happened to spot someone make a delivery to the back gates of the research facility as he was passing. At the time, he thought it was just something Mr Murston had wanted kept from the prying eyes of his wife, but after a few enquiries at the delivery service office with a rather friendly cashier, he managed to procure the shipping notice. He tracked down the Inker on the pretence of being a potential client, and while the Inker was preparing a sample for him in another room, he saw several vials of ink made up ready to be shipped. One slipped its way into his pocket, and when he compared it to the ink used for the set of scales, he found they were one and the same.'

She flicked through another few pages. 'Now here's where it gets really interesting. There's an entry on September the first: "While in the library, taking a short break from my work, I happened to come across a book on cases of 'rogue' Wytches throughout the ages (as though they aren't already rogue enough, with their ability to defy the laws of Alkemy to achieve what, at current, seems to be the impossible). Suitably intrigued by what the author deemed to be a 'rogue', I came across a tale called 'The Nekromancer', a Wytch who had tried to cross her magic with Alkemy to play with the line between life and death, in the hope of returning those who are lost back to life. Of course, it was a fantastical tale, but what caught my eye was an illustration of the Wytch's signature: a simple line drawing of a set of scales with one black circle and one white circle. It was nearly identical to the one I have been trying to track down, and the article mentioned that other Wytches throughout history tried to follow in this 'Nekromancer's' footsteps and had adopted her signature. So now the question is: what would a Nekromancer have to do with the Super Notes? Is it possible that the apparitions I saw when they were burnt were somehow once real people? The thought chills me to the core, but as the only line of investigation I have, I must pursue it. As the stamping ink is being delivered to the gates of this very facility, I feel I must now keep my enquires secret in case I am delving into far more dangerous circumstances than I originally thought.'"

The room was silent. The theory that Winkit had come up with initially had now been proven by Mr Edwards. Someone had adopted the title of Nekromancer and the Super Notes were likely a result of their activities. 'So, er, what did Mr Edwards do after that?' Johnathan managed to ask, though his whole body was trembling. The Super Notes that he'd touched and spoken of so frivolously might actually be people, or at least what was left of them after whatever foul experimentation they might have come under. It was enough to make him sick. He also couldn't help but count himself lucky that he'd never written on one himself, having always asked potential customers to use their own handwriting for his demonstrations, as that appeared to be what triggered the notes to activate their energy-draining ability.

'Well, he surmised that a Nekromancer would need either people or fresh bodies to experiment on, and so began looking into cases of missing persons and mysterious deaths; hence, those three reports there and that newspaper article.' Erin said, pointing them out.

The reports were all for men, and curiously, although they all had different professions, they had the same hobby of sculpting. The clipping, however, was of a girl who'd been gravely injured in a motor carriage accident, only to die in hospital a few days later from a completely unrelated illness.

Winkit squinted at the name. 'Aiyanna Dewfallow. Aiyanna ... now where have I heard that name before?'

'It's certainly an unusual name. Was she the Wytch of one of your familiar friends?' Jasmine asked, looking at the girl's photograph in the clipping. She had soft eyes and hair as dark as Jasmine's own.

'No, it's *too* unusual for a Wytch. Don't forget, our mistresses have such a bad reputation thanks to the Board of Alkemists that they try not to draw attention to themselves. Still, I know I've heard that name, and recently too.'

'Well, I've never heard it,' Molly said, 'so it can't have been anyone mentioned by Mother or Father. It must have been mentioned by someone connected with one of you lot,' she continued, nodding to the others.

Samuel raised an eyebrow. '*Our* lot? We have names, Miss Prim,' he sneered. 'Anyway, those missing men are more important than the girl.'

'How so?' Chester asked.

'Because, stupid, they all have the same connection to each other.'

'I don't—'

'Sculpting, idiot. Don't you remember what Erin's father told us? His top Alkemical Sculptor disappeared two months ago without a trace. And look at the dates on these reports. These men all disappeared *before* him, weeks apart from each other. Someone's kidnapping them,' Samuel said, exasperated. 'So, either they want an enormous statue, or the first three weren't good enough!'

'Good enough for what? What would a Nekromancer want with an Alkemical Sculptor?' Chester asked bluntly.

'How should I know?' Samuel shouted, and at the same time, Winkit jumped up.

'I've got it!' she exclaimed. 'I know where I've heard the name!' The others looked at her, curious, and Samuel and Chester forgot their quarrel. 'It was this afternoon at Mr Murston's house! Aiyanna is his niece! Her name was the code to the safe!'

'Another connection to the research facility. This really points the finger at them,' Jasmine said, shaking her head.

'Actually, I think it does just the opposite,' Erin declared. 'Why would my father orchestrate the kidnapping of his top Alkemical Sculptor when he needed him so desperately for the new motor carriage casing? And if Aiyanna was the code to Mr Murston's safe, then he obviously cared about her. I can't see him letting her intentionally die from a disease when she survived the accident.'

'Then if the facility isn't involved, where does that leave us?' Johnathan asked, perplexed.

'We carry on Mr Edwards' line of enquiry. Look for any recent missing persons cases, sudden illnesses or deaths. Anything at all that could be the work of this Nekromancer.'

'I hate to say this, Erin, but those kinds of records aren't readily available, especially now that your father is probably on the hunt for us,' Chester said solemnly. 'We'd have to have access to the hospital and police station, for a start.'

Beside him, Molly glowed with self-importance. 'I don't know about the police station, but I can probably get you into the hospital. Don't forget, my family own it.'

Johnathan cast her a sceptical look. 'You really think they'll just let us in because we know you?'

'I didn't say that. But I do have an idea to stop them being suspicious. Every few months, my parents give tours to potential medical students – they don't just own the hospital, they're qualified Doktors too. If you all pretended to be students interested in future careers at the hospital, then I *might* be able to get your names added to the list for the next tour. The least I could do is try.'

CHAPTER 11

*M*artha Aqua regarded her daughter's earnest expression pensively. They were sitting in the dining room, having just finished breakfast. Light filtered in from the icy windows and cast shadows from the silver water jug and porcelain bowls, shading much of the newspaper Martha had been reading before Molly had spoken up. Her husband, Phillip, had been out all night on duty, and had rushed from the room after only a few bites to catch up on his sleep. Now the two of them were alone.

It was unusual for Molly to linger after she'd eaten; normally she chose to hide until her first tutor of the morning lost patience and went looking for her. And she had certainly never shown an interest in the workings of the hospital, or medicine, despite all their attempts to engage her. Yet now she wanted to help with the tour for prospective medical students? Was she even familiar enough with it to know her way around? After all, the only period of her life when she'd spent any serious amount of time there was when they'd first adopted her, but she'd been an infant. The only other instances were brief check-ups, which had always taken place in the same section.

'I know what you're thinking, Mother.' Molly said, putting on a slight pout. 'You don't think I'm well enough acquainted with the hospital to be any help.'

'I wouldn't put it that way,' Martha said evenly. 'We always need people at the back of the tour to make sure no one gets lost. What I'm more curious about is why you've asked to take part. We've been giving the students tours for years, but you've never wanted to join us before.'

'I just ... wanted to do something different besides sitting through another one of Mr Aster's history lectures,' Molly replied. 'Not that I dislike history, of course,' she added hastily.

'I should hope not. Mr Aster is a fine tutor, and the history of Nodnol and the rest of D'nalg Ne is very important for your education. But I suppose a change every so often is not a bad idea.'

'Then you'll let me help? Really?'

'Yes, as long as you realise that this is a serious task and not a chance for you to simply skip around without learning anything. You will be in charge of seeing to the list of attending students. Interested parties have already put their names in the notice box outside the main entrance. They need to be counted and each person's experience taken note of. We have limited spaces on each tour, so make sure no one with less than three years of medical study is offered a place. See to it that the Knurse at reception has all the details so she can check everyone in as they arrive. Think you can do that?'

'Of course I can,' Molly said with a smile on her lips.

Martha's eyes lingered on her suspiciously. That smile looked far too mischievous to be sincere. Still, this might possibly be the only opportunity she'd have to open Molly's eyes to the benefits of working in medicine. If she said anything about it, the girl would probably lose interest. Better to stay quiet and let things play out.

～

'I can't believe we're doing this. Lying about who we are *again*,' Chester said dismally as they headed through the crowded city centre to the hospital. It had been a week since they'd escaped the research facility, and they had spent that time laying low, recovering from the whole ordeal. Molly had already sent word, by way of a fully healed Winkit, that she'd spoken to her parents and arranged for them to join the tour that morning.

'At least we don't have to dress up again. Medical students are usually our age anyway when they first get started at the hospital. Alfred and I used to work closely with them at the shop to help them understand what goes into making the remedies they prescribe,' Johnathan said brightly, falling into step beside him.

This time, Samuel and Erin had stayed at home; Samuel because the swelling from the blow to his head still hadn't gone down and he'd also managed to catch a cold, and Erin because she was the one most likely to be recognised if her father had sent people out to look for her. Not to mention the fact that the children had complained heavily the moment she even suggested going out.

'Besides, Chester, why does going around in disguise bother you when you have no quarrel with stealing?'

'Chester does have a quarrel with stealing,' Jasmine said, next to him. 'When we first came up with the idea of putting people to sleep with the instruments so we could sneak in, he refused to play his violin for a week. We did try it without him, but the sleep-inducing effect the instruments have doesn't work unless all four instruments are played together. We think that the Wytch who enchanted them preferred ensembles rather than solo players. Still, when we came back emptyhanded, and we and the children went hungry for a few days, he gave in and agreed to help.'

'On the terms that I'm never the one who has to take the loot from the house myself,' Chester said firmly.

'Fortunately, that's never been a problem because Sam has always wanted to do it. Talk about polar opposites,' she smirked.

Johnathan grinned; the brothers really were different to each other. He shivered and pulled up the collar of his coat to try and warm his freezing ears, a thought occurring to him. 'Why do the instruments never put you four to sleep?'

Jasmine shrugged. 'I suppose whatever enchantment is on them allows for the players to be unaffected. Having instruments that lull people to sleep isn't much use if the musicians fall asleep while they're playing, is it?'

The snow was unrelenting that morning, raining

down in heavy flurries, and as they arrived at the hospital, it obscured their vision so much that Johnathan accidently walked into the double glass doors of the entrance.

Jasmine snorted in such an unladylike way that several passers-by stared at her, but she ignored them and pushed Johnathan aside so that she could grasp the vertical handle and heave the door open.

They went in, glad of the immediate warmth from the twin Kerical heaters by the reception desk. 'Good morning,' Johnathan greeted the Knurse filling papers there. 'We're prospective students and have our names down for today's tour.'

The Knurse studied them. 'Ah, yes. Young Miss Aqua did tell me you would be arriving shortly.'

Johnathan made a slight, strangled sound. 'Molly's here?'

'Yes, it seems she has finally taken an interest in what her parents do. I believe she will be helping out with the tour itself, to make sure there are no stragglers. This is a big hospital and we *have* had people on the tour go missing a few times. They always turned up in the end, but one year we had a girl who got lost in the boils-and-sores ward and wound up getting locked in the dirty laundry room. The smell from those towels covered in popped pustules and the oozing plasma from septic rashes can get a bit heady at times, and the poor girl was in there for hours. It took her several days to recover, if I'm to believe her mother's complaints.'

Johnathan didn't blame her. Just hearing the story made him feel unwell.

'Now, I'll just mark your names off my list, and you can go and join the others in the waiting room,' the Knurse continued, picking up a thick visitors' book.

'Ah, yes. It's Johnathan, Chester, and Jasmine,' Johnathan told her.

'Lovely.' She placed a tick next to their names on the list. Then she frowned. 'I've got two more names on here. Were there supposed to be others with you?'

Of course, Molly would have told her that Samuel and Erin would be coming too. 'Oh, sorry. We forgot to mention that our friends have come down with the flu. They send their apologies,' he said solemnly.

'Not to worry, we've already got a large group this morning, so perhaps it's for the best. Now, off you go; Doktors Aqua and Aqua should be with you soon.' She waved them off to the right, where they went through a stark white door leading into the waiting room.

She certainly hadn't been lying. The room was full of students their own age, all whispering excitedly to each other. With this many people, leaving the tour unnoticed would be easy, especially with Molly helping.

Some of them raised their heads as the three entered, but most carried on talking. They had separated themselves into friendship groups, so to Johnathan, Chester and Jasmine's delight, it didn't look as though they were expected to try and mingle.

After five minutes of eavesdropping, and Jasmine complaining that everyone sounded dull, the doors to the waiting room opened and a tall man and slightly shorter woman entered, both sporting bright blonde hair. They wore surprisingly shabby white coats, with pockets full of thermometers, bandages, stethoscopes, and other medical instruments with names Johnathan couldn't confidently pronounce.

Molly stood next to them, clothed in a plain white dress and her hair done up in a tight, clinical style bun. It made her look much older than her twelve years.

'Greetings, ladies and gentlemen,' her father said, addressing the whole room with a warm, rounded voice. 'Welcome to Phlamel Hospital, the heart of Nodnol's medical care, and home to the most efficient medical training currently available. My name is Doktor Aqua, as is my wife's.' He indicated Molly's mother, who smiled at everyone with an almost glowing set of teeth. 'But as that tends to get confusing, for the purposes of this tour, you may address us by our first names, Phillip and Martha.

'Now, I'm sure you all have lots of questions, but please save them for the end when we shall have a brief discussion back here with a breakdown of what to expect when training at this hospital. We'll start the tour with the wards on this level first, which covers diseases of the blood, nerve disorders, and an accident clinic. The other levels have a far greater variety of wards, but we do a great deal of filing down here too, which, as I'm sure you'll be saddened to hear, is also a part of our jobs.' He gestured for everyone to follow him through the doors.

Molly hung back to wait for Johnathan and the others, and then walked with them behind the rest of the crowd. 'I'm glad to see you got here on time. By the state of you when I left last week, I was worried I'd be going through all this trouble for nothing.' She rooted around in one of her pockets, giving a smile to a Knurse passing them in the hall, and once she was clear, handed Johnathan a key.

'What's this for?' he asked.

'It's for getting into the filing rooms. Father usually carries it on his person, but during tours he never needs to use it, so I pinched it from his jacket pocket as we were headed down here to meet everyone. Some of the filing rooms also have a combination lock too, but luckily my parents are sentimental and always use the date they got married. I've written it here for you.' She handed him a folded sheet of paper.

'Thank you, Molly. We wouldn't be able to do this without you,' he said gratefully.

'I know. And I wouldn't be doing it if Winkit didn't trust you so much,' she replied. 'There's one important thing you need to remember, though. The key must be back in Father's pocket by the time the tour ends, because when I asked around, I found out that his midday inspection always starts in the filing rooms. You've got about two hours, okay?'

He, Chester and Jasmine all nodded.

'Good. As soon as we turn into the first ward, you need to go in the opposite direction. If anyone stops you, tell them you're just going to the bathroom,' Molly advised.

The tour had reached the first wards. Her father gave a short rundown of the current patients and how they were being treated, and led the way in. Molly gave the signal, and Johnathan, Chester and Jasmine turned around and headed for the filing rooms.

As it turned out, they were stopped by three Knurses and two other Doktors, but when they gave the explanation Molly had told them, everyone went away without question.

Fortunately, the main filing room door was hidden behind a trolley full of clean bedding, so no one could see as they turned the key in the lock and crept inside. 'Lock it back up,' Jasmine said as soon as she'd closed the door. 'I don't want anyone else coming in here to disturb us.'

As Johnathan did so Chester found a Kerical lamp to light the rows and rows of filing cabinets now before them. Their eyes widened. 'Where ... do you think we should start?' Chester ventured.

'I have no idea,' Johnathan murmured. The room was three times the size of his apartment and there was a door on either side, leading to rooms containing further files.

Jasmine took a good look at the cabinet directly in front of them. The drawers were organised by illness, with patients stored alphabetically inside. 'These are all for patients who are still alive. If our Nekromancer needs bodies, the morgue records will probably be our best bet. They should tell us when the patients died and which undertakers the bodies were taken to.'

'But what sort of time period are we looking for?' Chester asked.

'Well, I would say anything from this year, but that girl Aiyanna died two years ago, and if Mr Edwards thought her death was relevant, then we should take that into account, too,' she explained.

Working individually, they checked every cabinet for one labelled as files for the morgue, but it was nowhere to be seen. 'It has to be in one of the other rooms,' Johnathan said. He looked at the others. 'How much time do we have left?'

Jasmine and Chester glanced at each other. 'We

thought you were the one keeping track of the time,' Chester said, his brow creasing.

Johnathan cursed. 'Never mind, we'll have to keep going and hope we finish before the tour ends.' He ran over to the door on the righthand side. It had a combination lock as Molly had warned so, taking the paper from his pocket, he turned the dials to the correct digits. The lock clicked open. 'Here,' he said, turning back. 'You go through the other door and see if it's in there. This is the code.' He gave Jasmine the paper and then went into the next room.

The cabinets there were thinner and on some of them the drawers were so rusted that he wasn't even sure they would open. He checked the labels. None of them read 'Morgue', but he thought they might be useful all the same. They contained files on every Doktor and Knurse who had worked at the hospital since its founding, and one of the cabinets had a drawer marked specifically for dismissed staff.

That particular drawer was the rustiest of the lot, but after a few minutes of tugging and kicking, it sprang open. The names were all ordered by employment date and only one was listed as having been in the last ten years. He pulled it out, careful not to drop any of its contents, and flicked through it. It belonged to a Doktor Ichabod Cornell; he'd certainly had quite the career, for his file was full of achievements and promotions. Why then would someone so accomplished have been dismissed?

He checked the file's back cover and stapled to it was a breakdown of all the Doktor's indiscretions, year by year. The first few years were fairly trivial – bad bedside manner, untidiness – but listed just before he was dismissed a year and a half ago were twenty cases of patient negligence, and for each one, how the patient had died.

'Johnathan! Johnathan, we've found it!' Chester called from the other room.

Quickly, Johnathan shut the cabinet, keeping the file out, and headed over to where Chester and Jasmine were waiting. The room they were in was smaller than the one he'd just left, but still there were cabinets filling every inch of space. The morgue's files were dedicated to the whole back wall and Jasmine had located all the ones stating the time period they needed. One of the drawers was still open where Jasmine had been searching through it.

'Take a look at these!' She thrust a wad of files at him and he nearly dropped the one on Doktor Cornell. Impatiently, she began opening them for him, pointing out their dates of death and the undertaker that they were all supposed to have been taken to. 'None of them were ever sent to the same place, but for every one of them there's a note from the undertaker declaring that the bodies never arrived when they were supposed to. They all turned up weeks later, half decayed, and with cuts and markings that have nothing to do with their illness. There's even one body that was *never* found!'

'And guess who it was? Aiyanna Dewfallow!' Chester said triumphantly.

'Yes, yes,' Jasmine said, waving a hand at him. 'That's not the most important part. What we discovered was that all of these people had the same Doktor, a Doktor—'

'Ichabod Cornell, by any chance?' Johnathan cut in. He showed them the file, and they compared it with all the information in the patients' files.

'Is this ... *him*, then? Our Nekromancer? Winkit said that they weren't always Wytches, didn't she?' Chester queried.

'Yes, she did,' Jasmine confirmed. 'If he is our Nekromancer, then all we have to do now is find him.'

'Why do I have the feeling it won't be that simple?' Johnathan mumbled. Yet he was glad that for all their troubles, they were actually on to something! He sighed with relief, but then remembered the time. 'We've got to re-join the tour before it ends!'

In a flurry of papers, they tidied up the rooms as best they could and locked the side doors. They still had the files they'd found with them, ready to show Erin and Samuel when they got back to the house and, unsurprisingly, Jasmine managed to fit most of them into the pockets of her vest, with the rest stuffed into Johnathan's inside coat pocket.

Then, as silently and inconspicuously as possible, they exited the filing room and snuck back along the corridors to find the tour. Unfortunately, they met them coming around the corner from the main stairwell, and Johnathan ran headlong into Martha Aqua, knocking her to the ground.

CHAPTER 12

'*Y*oung man, if we have but one rule at this hospital, it is to *always look where you're going,*' Molly's mother scolded as she scooped herself up off the floor and dusted down her white coat. 'Have you any idea how dangerous it is to simply go running about? These halls can get extremely busy. What would you have done if you'd have knocked over a patient? An elderly woman with a broken hip, or a child with extensive respiratory problems?'

'I'm terribly sorry, Doktor Aqua, but I was just so eager to join back in after—' Johnathan began quickly, pulling his most apologetic expression.

'After what? Why were you separated from the rest of the group?' she demanded, her eyes searching his. In the commotion, Chester and Jasmine had seamlessly merged with the other teenagers, so no one realised that they had been missing too.

Molly stepped forwards in a move to simultaneously save Johnathan from bumbling his reply and discreetly take the key back from him. 'I'm afraid it was my fault, Mother. I agreed to let him go to the bathroom, as long as he came straight back.'

Martha Aqua scrutinised her daughter, but Molly kept her expression passive. 'We have bathroom facilities on every floor. Why would he have found it necessary to use the ones down here?'

'They were occupied – all of them – and I was desperate,' Johnathan lied, looking every bit as embarrassed as he sounded. There were sniggers around the group, and one or two were openly laughing.

'As unlikely as that sounds, I suppose we have no choice but to accept what you say,' Phillip Aqua said, standing by his wife. 'Though, if we were not on such a tight schedule, I might be inclined to investigate. Then again, I'm no stranger to the anxiety that a full bladder can create. In fact, I believe it was only last week that I had to use the ladies to—'

'That's quite enough chatter, dear,' Martha Aqua said hastily amidst an onslaught of snorting from everyone. 'I suggest you fall back amongst the group, young man, and *try* not to disappear between here and the waiting room.'

~

An hour later Johnathan, Chester and Jasmine arrived back at the house. The talk from Martha and Phillip Aqua had bored them nearly to tears, and once they'd been dismissed, it had taken all their self-control not to run from the building.

When they walked into the hall, Samuel met them looking decidedly drained. 'I hope you had fun while I was here dying,' he said sourly.

'You look perfectly healthy to me. I can't even *see*

that horrendous bump on your head anymore,' Jasmine said sweetly. 'And we didn't force you to stay here, you chose to. Now, where's Erin? We've got some news.'

'She's in the living room, treating a few of the children for hiccups. They begged us for ice-cream, and because Erin's been so down about having to keep out of sight lately, she relented and went out to get some. But they ate it so fast that they ended up with hiccup fits.'

'Erin went shopping?' Chester asked, incredulous. 'And you *let* her? Why didn't you offer to go yourself?'

'As I said, I spent the day *dying*; if not from the river of mucus running from my nose and the headache I had this morning, then definitely from boredom and the requests to sing nursery rhymes a hundred times. Besides, it's Erin. I wasn't going to try and stop her from doing something she'd already decided to do. She'd bite my head off.'

'And I was perfectly alright.' Erin stood in the living room doorway. Her face was drawn, but her eyes had an alert brightness that Johnathan usually associated with excess amounts of coffee. 'I was careful,' she added when they looked at her sceptically, 'I only went to the corner shop on Arnvile Road. It's fifteen minutes away from here if you take all the short cuts that I did. I was nowhere near the city centre.'

'Are you sure you weren't seen?' Johnathan pressed. 'I mean, if your father wanted to have you watched instead of trying to capture you, then his spies would hardly make it obvious, would they? For all we know, you might have been followed back here.'

'Come on, Johnathan, don't you think I've thought of that? I know how my father works, and I *wasn't* seen. Besides, just because I'm the most easily recognisable since I resemble my parents doesn't mean that they aren't out looking for you, too. We *all* have to be careful.' At that moment, a small girl appeared beside her. Erin smiled at her. 'Are you feeling better now?' she asked.

The girl gave a small nod, then caught sight of Johnathan. She stared at him, and then glanced at Samuel, before looking back at Erin. Grinning toothily, she said in a loud sing-song voice, 'Erin loves Johnathan!' and ran back into the living room, where much giggling was heard.

Erin blushed, rounding on Samuel. 'Just what have you been telling them?' she hissed.

Samuel shrugged. 'Nothing. They asked me what you like to dream about, and I mentioned that you said Johnathan's name in your sleep last night, that's all.'

'Samuel!' she growled

'Perhaps we should discuss what we found out at the hospital,' Chester cut in as Erin took off a shoe to throw at his brother.

Reluctantly, she put it back on. 'I suppose we should,' she said curtly. 'Let's go into the kitchen. I'll make tea.'

Once she had calmed down, Chester, Jasmine and Johnathan told her and Samuel about the bodies that had arrived at the undertaker's several weeks later than expected, and how Doktor Cornell had been responsible for all of their deaths through negligence. Finally, they revealed that Aiyanna Dewfallow's body had never turned up at all.

'So based on all of this, I think we can assume that Doktor Cornell is the most likely suspect to be our Nekromancer. If we can find him, perhaps we can force him to tell us what the Super Notes are and why they appear to be the cause of the sudden Acute Energy Loss outbreak,' Johnathan finished.

Erin studied Doktor Cornell's file. 'There *is* an address listed for him here. I don't expect for one moment that he's still there; if he wanted to lie low and carry out his experiments with Aiyanna's body, he wouldn't stay somewhere so close to prying eyes. But it's a start. When shall we leave?'

'Erin—'

'Don't repeat yourself, Johnathan. My mind is made up. I'm going with you this time. And since he's been complaining all day, Samuel can come with us,' she said, glowering in Samuel's direction.

'I don't think all of us should be out at the same time,' Chester said. 'The children won't like it.'

'We won't be. You and Jasmine will stay with them for the afternoon. Winkit's here too, but as they were playing with her all morning, she's resting now, so try not to let them disturb her too much.'

Seeing that it was pointless arguing, Chester and Jasmine resigned themselves to their childminding duties while the other three got ready to leave. The Doktor's house was located in a part of the city that none of them were familiar with, so Erin dug out an old map of Nodnol and spread it out on the table.

'I'm sure it's to the west,' Johnathan said, scouring the tangle of lines representing streets and running over them with his fingers. 'One of my old clients at the shop used to live there; she said the river runs right through it.' He located the blue line of the river and followed it in the direction of its source. 'Yes, here it is. The green district. Some of the finest seaweed powder is made there. Excellent for treating colds when mixed with Arred residue.'

'*Wonderful*, you tell me that *now*.' Samuel clapped his hands together and looked at Johnathan in mocking admiration.

Johnathan ignored him.

'It shouldn't be hard to get there if we take the backstreets,' Erin said, plotting the route with her fingers. 'Are you ready?'

'I think so,' Johnathan replied and, without waiting for Samuel to catch up, they headed out through the door.

~

The smell in the green district was atrocious, but because of the high concentration of salt in the air from being so close to the river, there was delightfully less snow than in the rest of the city.

However, the constant fishing, drying and grinding of seaweed in the area had permanently stained the ground a dark green, making it look like the whole place was covered in lichen. The houses were cramped and a large majority of them were made of wood. Despite its reputation for quality seaweed powder, it appeared to be a very poor part of the city.

'I'd have thought with a Doktor's wage, that Cornell could have afforded a place somewhere nicer,' Samuel observed, watching a woman empty a chamber pot from her top window.

'Not if he was spending his Ren on something

else, as we suspect. I don't know what kind of apparatus one needs to attempt to bring back the dead, but I'm sure it doesn't come cheap,' Erin put in. She checked the map again. 'His house should be right past this tackle shop.'

They came to a stop a few minutes later, outside number seventy-seven. The white paint on the window frames was peeling, and an evil-smelling brown smear decorated the front door.

'That's not what I think it is, is it?' Samuel asked, his eyes bulging.

'Probably not, no,' Johnathan laughed. 'It looks like river mud to me. That always has a pungent odour, and if you look closely, you'll see the tell-tale green flecks of seaweed in it. I'm glad it's not on the handle, though. Regardless of what it is, I'd rather not touch it.' He turned to Erin. 'It looks like you were right, Cornell certainly doesn't live here anymore, and I don't think anyone else would ever want to. It's practically falling apart.'

Putting on a brave face, he turned the handle. The door was stiff where the wood was swollen with moisture, but a good kick loosened it enough to open it. Inside, the floor was bare boards riddled with woodworm holes and boot polish stains. Decorating the hall was a coatrack with a single mildew-covered jacket and a crooked bookshelf displaying a few cloth-bound tomes which, on close inspection, were books on Alkemical theory and Kerical engineering. Interesting, but nothing that would help them locate Cornell himself. Johnathan searched the pockets of the decaying jacket, but they contained nothing save a list of groceries scribbled in a hand so slanted, it was barely legible.

They peered into a joint living room and kitchen, where they saw only a sofa with protruding springs, a wooden table, an assortment of pots and pans, and a rusty stove. 'It doesn't look like he left much behind,' Erin said grimly as they checked the whole room for any insight into the Doktor's life.

Moving on to the bedroom, which contained a wardrobe with approximately a year's worth of laundry receipts inside, and a bare iron bed frame, Johnathan couldn't help but think they were wasting their time.

The last room to check was the bathroom, where the state of the toilet was enough to send Samuel running. Johnathan and Erin chose to ignore it and examined the contents of the medicine cabinet. A broken toothbrush was all that was inside, but the shelf it rested on had come loose; the screws fixing it to the brackets on the inside of the cabinet were rusted to the point of becoming dust, making it slant to the side. There was a rough patch behind it, as though a chunk of the wall had been cut out and then repaired.

'What do you suppose that is?' Erin traced her fingers across it.

Johnathan shrugged. 'I've got no idea.' He tapped it with his knuckles, and the sound it made was decidedly hollow. 'I think there's a gap behind it. I wonder if we can scrape this bit off and get through.'

'Give me a moment,' Erin said quickly and disappeared back down the hall.

Meanwhile, Johnathan tried scraping at the uneven area with his apartment key. It made a slight mark, but nothing significant enough to make him think he could break through any time soon. He was just about to look for something else that might work when there was a shout behind him.

'Johnathan, stand aside!'

Jumping out of the way, the heavy base of the coatrack whipped past his nose and crashed into the cabinet, which split apart completely from the impact. As the remains clattered to the floor, Johnathan saw that the rough patch had crumbled away, revealing a small hole as they'd suspected.

Next to him, Erin put the coatrack down, looking enormously pleased with herself. 'I was hoping that would work,' she said breathlessly.

Johnathan swallowed. 'Perhaps next time, you could give me slightly more warning.'

'You reacted well enough,' she replied, unable to conceal her smirk. 'Anyway, shall we investigate this hole?' Without waiting for an answer, she reached into the crumbling opening and felt about. Within seconds, her eyes lit up triumphantly and she pulled her hand back, slowly unfurling her fist. On her palm was a single, dirt encrusted key. Taking it over to the small sink in the corner, she washed the filth away.

Now clean, they saw that it was silver, stamped with a miniature set of scales complete with black and white circles. The symbol of the Nekromancer.

'Well, if this isn't proof that the Doktor was at least connected with this Nekromancer, then I don't know what is,' Johnathan murmured. 'Do you think it's for a safe?'

'No, most safes nowadays have a combination lock, and even if one did still need a key, what would be the point of sealing it up inside a wall? It's hardly practical to get to regularly,' she mused. 'Let's check outside. There's a small garden around the back. Who knows what could be lurking out there?'

Locating Samuel, who was recovering in the kitchen, they went outside and down the narrow alley beside the house. The garden was a square area paved with cream-coloured slabs and, in the centre, completely out of place, was a well. Its circular wall was solidly built and a handle jutted from the side of its beam so that the hook dangling from it could be raised and lowered. A tin bucket, left there so long that moss had grown around it, rested on the edge.

Samuel leaned over the wall and looked down. 'It must be deep, I can't even see the bottom.' Building up his saliva, he spat down the shaft, counting the seconds until it hit the water. It never did. 'Dry,' he said, turning to Erin and Johnathan. But his arm caught the bucket and sent it crashing down into the well. When it hit the bottom, there was a distinct clang of metal on metal.

They stared at each other. 'I'm no expert, but I've never heard of a well with a metal bottom,' Johnathan said.

'Neither have I,' Erin agreed. 'What on earth could be down there, do you think?'

'I know one way to find out,' Samuel said, tugging on the rope to see how strong it was. It seemed sturdy enough, and the beam it was attached to didn't even budge 'Do you have a Kerical lantern with you?'

Erin shook her head. 'I did notice that the tackle shop next door sells candle-lit ones though. But I don't have any Ren with me.'

Johnathan rooted through his pockets. He felt several coins clinking together, and the crisp touch of a ten Ren note. 'I've got some. Give me a second and I'll go and fetch one.'

He dashed to the tackle shop, breezing in and out so quickly that the owner barely had time to register his presence and accept the payment hastily dropped onto the counter.

When he returned to the garden, holding a lantern, fresh candles and a box of matches, he found Erin helping to tie the rope around Samuel's waist. She finished it with a knot Johnathan had once seen demonstrated by Alfred when he'd explained how he'd often gone sailing by the coast in his youth. It was supposed to be the most secure knot possible.

'That should do it,' she announced as Johnathan set up the lantern. 'Are you sure you want to go down there? It looks awfully claustrophobic.'

'That's why I have to,' Samuel replied. 'I'm the smallest, so I'll have the most room to move around. Besides, I'm not so sure this rope could even *take* your weight,' he said slyly, but she was so concerned about his safety that she didn't react. Samuel rolled his eyes. 'Come on Johnathan, hand me the lantern and let's get started. This rope's like a corset, I don't want to spend all day in it.'

Lantern in hand, Samuel gave a thumbs up and Johnathan and Erin turned the well's handle to lower him to the bottom.

Down and down he went, until the top of the well was only a small circle of light above him. Holding his lantern so that its light spread as far as possible, Samuel could see that the shaft was dry and encrusted with years of solidified slime, but so far it was everything he expected a normal dry well to be.

It was only when the bottom finally came into

view that he understood why the bucket had sounded like it had hit metal. The bottom of the well wasn't a bottom at all, it was a hatch, engraved with the set of scales symbol just like the key.

'Erin! Johnathan!'

There was a faint response from above.

'I think you'll like what I've just found!'

*T*wo metres from the hatch, the shaft of the well opened out so that there was enough space for several people to stand in.

Samuel tugged three times on the rope that was binding him. There was a pause in his lowering and then he started being hauled back to the top of the well. When he emerged into the sunlight, he practically jumped over the wall in excitement, trying to tell Johnathan and Erin what he'd seen before they'd finished turning the well's handle.

'Slow down, Samuel,' Erin said swiftly. 'You're burbling like a small child, and I can't make any sense of it.'

Samuel took a deep breath and started again. 'What I *said* was that there's a metal hatch down there in a space easily wide enough for the three of us to get to. It's got that weird symbol on it too, so it's definitely linked to Cornell. It's not rusty or anything either, so together we could probably get it open. You have to come down there with me and see it.'

'We can't all go down there,' she pointed out. 'We can only be lowered one at a time, and there'd be no-one left to help lower the last person. I don't think any of us feel like risking our lives by climbing down the rope unaided, either. And even if we did somehow manage to overcome that, we have no idea where the hatch leads. How would we get back again?'

Samuel huffed. 'You always have to be so logical, don't you?' he complained. 'Alright then, if only two of us can go down, who's going to stay behind to make sure we don't get lost forever?'

'I will, I'm not that good in enclosed spaces. But I have my reservations about letting you loose down there, Samuel. It could be dangerous and I don't want you to go charging off into anything that we're not ready for,' she cautioned.

Johnathan grinned. 'Don't worry, I'll keep an eye on him for you,' he said.

Samuel scowled. 'I'm only slightly younger than you, you know, and I do *not* need babysitting. I can be perfectly sensible. *You're* the one I'm worried about. Molly told me that the thought of dead bodies gives you the willies,' he jeered, leaning closer. "What if we find some of those down there? All the remains of the people Cornell tried to bring back to life?'

'At least the sight of a dirty toilet doesn't make me scarper,' Johnathan bit back defensively. 'You ran out so fast that I thought you were training for a race.'

Erin tapped her foot, eyeing the darkening sky. 'Boys, if you're going to go exploring, then I suggest you stop arguing and get down there. It's nearly sunset and we've still got a long walk home.'

Feeling sheepish, Johnathan and Samuel split the candles and matches equally between them so that they'd both have some form of light. Then Samuel was lowered back down, with Johnathan a few minutes after him.

When he saw the size of the hatch, nearly filling the entire space at the bottom of the well, his eyes widened. It looked as though it had been professionally crafted, not just something cobbled together out of beaten metal to shield a secret hideout. Whatever Cornell had been up to, he'd taken it seriously.

The handle on the hatch was a bar that had to be twisted anti-clockwise to unlock the clamps holding the whole thing down. They had to move it together, for even though there was no rust as Samuel had mentioned, it was still heavy and stiff.

Once the clamps were off, they pulled the hatch open, wincing as it swung up on its hinges and clanged against the ground. It was a void of blackness inside, but by gingerly lowering the lantern Samuel could see that the light revealed a solid metal ladder welded to one side. One after the other, they climbed down it.

Johnathan sniffed. He couldn't see much yet because the light from Samuel's lantern only spread so far, and the boy was already several rungs below him. Sealed up for so long, he'd expected the air to be stale, but it wasn't; it was fresh. And that meant there was probably an air vent connecting to the surface.

By the time they came to the end of the ladder, their limbs were aching. Johnathan lit a candle so that he had his own light, and they began exploring. The floor was laid with neat tiles, though more than a few were cracked and chipped. Two long tables were in the centre of the chamber, the kind used by an undertaker when preparing a body for burial. On the far wall, after a quick perimeter search revealing that the chamber was shaped like a square, they saw a rack of metal instruments. It was an eclectic mix of scalpels, saws, knives, thin serrated discs, rope wire and chains. There was also a Kerical lamp, but when they tried to switch it on, it wouldn't work. Holding both candle and lantern up together to increase the light, they soon found out why: the circuits inside had all been disconnected.

'That's odd,' Johnathan commented. 'The way this has been cut looks like whoever did it wanted to cross-examine it to see how the normal Lectric responds to the Alkemical components to give out the light.'

Samuel snorted. 'We're in a room that looks like a weird clinical torture chamber and you say that's *odd*?' He shined the lantern over to the corners. 'What about those bones over there?'

At the word 'bones', Johnathan started, but he went over to them nonetheless. 'These are animal bones,' he said, examining one of the skulls with a grimace. 'Dogs and cats most likely.' He looked in the other corners, where he found more animal bones piled high.

'So, he swiped people's pets to experiment on?' Samuel asked, putting a hand inside one of the skulls and waving it about like a puppet. He spotted a jawbone and used it to make the skull look like it was speaking.

Johnathan turned away from him in disgust. 'Probably.' His eyes came to rest on a series of small holes at the bottom of one of the walls. He knelt, trying to see if they went through to the other side. But he couldn't angle his candle enough to see and ended up spilling hot wax on the floor in the process.

'Did you give Jasmine back her penknife the other day?' he asked suddenly.

'What made you bring that up?' Samuel shot back with a frown.

'Do you have the knife or not?'

'No, she snatched it back the moment we got home. Why?'

'Then pass me one of those long thin ones hanging up on the rack,' Johnathan said, gesturing. 'I think I've found something.'

Samuel fetched a knife as Johnathan had asked, making the rack clatter as he wriggled it free from the others. Handing it to him, he stood behind, holding out the lantern so Johnathan could see better.

The blade was narrow enough to fit one of the holes, and he pushed it through, right up to the hilt, wriggling it around just to make sure. The area behind was definitely hollow. He took the knife out again and checked the rest of the wall for any markings or something that might give a hint as to what was on the other side. Instead, he saw a seam, barely three hair's width, making a rectangle on the wall. Curious, he dug at it with the knife. It caught on the seam, revealing a slight lip. Using the knife as a lever, he put his weight into raising the lip up.

There was a loud grinding, as if an old mechanism had suddenly been spurred into action, and then the part of the wall Johnathan was examining moved forwards several inches and then slid to one side. He and Samuel gaped. Beyond, in the gap where the wall had been, was a tunnel, tiled all around with white porcelain squares.

With a quick glance at each other and then at the

ladder leading to the well, where Erin was still waiting, they headed inside.

Sconces lined the sides, Kerical ones, but these
had been taken apart like the lamp. Still, there looked
to be nothing dangerous in the tunnel, and the tiles
were so shiny that they carried the lantern light far-
ther than normal, meaning they had some idea of
what was immediately ahead.

Not that there was anything. The minutes passed,
but the tunnel went on and on. Eventually, they had
no choice but to turn back. They couldn't leave Erin
waiting there all night.

~

It was fully dark now and still the boys hadn't come
back. Erin's hands were freezing, she breathed on
them to warm them up, but it did no good.

She took out the silver key they'd found and
turned it in her hands. It reflected the moonlight well.
Once again, she tried to work out what it might be for,
but aside from the symbol, there were no other markings on it. With a discontented sniff, she put it away
and strolled around the garden.

If it had simply been windy rather than cold, she
would have been perfectly warm, because the wall
from the tackle shop next door was so high that it
completely cut off the howling air she could hear
raging in the streets.

A door banged close by. She jumped, but the
shouting of a woman at a man with extremely slurred
speech told her that it was only a drunkard returning
home late. She turned back to the well, leaning over it
and straining her eyes, searching for any sign of

lanternlight. She might as well have been looking into a bowl of ink.

Why were they so late? It had been hours. What could they possibly have found down there that would take them this long? An uncomfortable feeling settled in her stomach. What if something, or *someone*, had found them instead?

Should she make her way home and get Chester and Jasmine, and maybe even Winkit, to come back with her so they could search for them together? No. What if the boys were making their way back even now and wanted to be hauled up from the well? If she left, there would be no one to do it.

Another door banged, but this time she ignored it, too wrapped up in her thoughts to notice the men looking at her through the bathroom window of Cornell's house. They put their heads together, whispering, as she paced back and forth, the moon's light clearly highlighting her face.

They left and moments later crept down the alley to the garden. She heard a stone skip against the wall as one of them stumbled and turned in time to see them emerge from the shadows. She gasped, shrinking back against the tackle shop's wall, searching for an escape, but she knew there wasn't one, unless she wanted to jump down the well.

Despite her previous concerns about it, the thought was starting to sound very appealing. The rope had been fully drawn back up after Johnathan had untied himself below. If she kept a tight hold of it and used her legs as an anchor so that she didn't plummet to the bottom, perhaps she could abseil down and get away.

She made a run for it, charging at the well and

grabbing the rope, tearing her skirt as she climbed over the short wall. The men watched her attempt to lower herself down, but the moment she dropped out of sight, they caught the rope and hauled her back up.

One of them pulled out a knife. She screamed, but a hand was clamped firmly over her mouth. The man with the knife cut off a large section of the rope that his friend had prized from her hands, and together they used it to tie her up. With a last look around the garden, they covered Erin in a hessian sheet and left.

The climb up the ladder felt like it took even longer than the descent, and when they reached the hatch door and climbed into the well, Samuel's lantern began sputtering. Johnathan took a fresh candle from his pocket and lit it, replacing the lantern's spent one so that they didn't lose their light.

'Erin!' he bellowed. 'Erin, can you hear us?' There was no response. 'Maybe she went back into the house?'

'What for?' Samuel asked. 'We already checked everything in there. It's as bare as a newborn's—'

'She might have needed the bathroom,' Johnathan said mildly, deliberately cutting him off.

'In *that* toilet? Please, even if she was desperate, she would have found somewhere else to go rather than use that.'

'Then she might have fallen asleep. We're all tired; the only reason I'm still awake is because I've spent the last few hours having to put up with you,' Johnathan quipped.

'Thanks,' Samuel replied acidly. 'Nice to know I'm useful.' He took a deep breath, and as loud as he could, shouted, 'ERIN!' Again, nothing, except the startled squeaking of a mouse by their feet. Samuel sighed. 'What do we do now?'

'We'll have to wait. She can't be far away; she wouldn't just up and leave us like that,' Johnathan replied. At least he didn't think so.

'I don't know. We have been gone for a long time.' Samuel sat down against the dry wall. 'What if she got worried and went to get the others?'

Johnathan didn't answer. He was starting to think that they shouldn't have gone exploring at all that night. If they'd left it until the morning, when they could have gone down in broad daylight, perhaps Erin might have stayed at home and Chester and Jasmine come with them instead. That way there would have been two waiting and two exploring, the smart thing to do considering the situation.

They waited for another half an hour and then tried calling again. When she didn't respond that time, they started to panic. 'You don't think someone saw us walk down to the green district earlier, do you?' Samuel asked, rubbing his stiff legs.

'You mean someone working for Erin's father?' Johnathan ventured. 'I hope not; we were careful with the route we chose.'

'But what if someone did? What if someone followed us to this house, and saw Erin standing there on her own?'

Johnathan studied his feet, feeling useless. 'The more I think about it, the more that seems the only explanation. But one thing's certain. If she's not up there, then we can't get out, at least not this way, and that means we have no way of helping her if she *is* in danger. We have to find out what's at the end of the tunnel. There must be another way up to the surface; that's the only reason for the air to be so clean.'

They looked back at the ladder and, with new determination, began the climb down once more.

CHAPTER 14

'We must have walked halfway across the city by now,' Samuel complained as he and Johnathan stopped to rest.

They were back in the tunnel leading from Doktor Cornell's secret underground room, and so far there had been no twists or turns, and no change of scenery. It was all one straight tiled path that gave no indication of stopping.

'Well, at least we should pop out somewhere familiar. By my reckoning, we're almost at the city centre,' Johnathan said.

'You mean, *if* we pop out? Why can't there be another hidden door somewhere around here?'

'There might be one yet. With these many tiles a seam or two is an easy thing to miss. For all we know, we might have walked passed it.' Johnathan tried not to smile as he spoke. He had checked all the way along for any such signs and had seen no indications of a doorway or even an air vent.

Samuel turned to him, a look of horror on his face. 'You mean to say that we've walked all this way for *nothing?*'

Johnathan couldn't help it, his mouth twitched up into a smirk. 'Don't worry, I've been searching the whole time. We haven't missed anything. But I think we might be coming to the end, or maybe a different section. Hold up your hand, palm out, and stand completely still.'

Samuel eyed him suspiciously but did it anyway. There was a slight tingle on his fingertips. 'The air's moving,' he said, awed.

'Exactly. And the only reason for that can be that there's a gap up ahead. Most likely a door.'

They walked for some minutes more before they came to the wall. It was grey stone, roughly shaped, as if it had once been part of a cave. There was a door set into it, a visible one this time, made of metal and clamped shut like the hatch had been with four iron clamps. They turned the handle anti-clockwise, expecting the clamps to shoot open as they had before, but only two of them did.

'Great. Another puzzle,' Samuel muttered, kicking the wall. The stone was solid, and it jarred his toes even through his shoes. Crying out in pain, he hopped around, trying to nurse them.

Johnathan didn't even see him; his thoughts were on the door and the remaining clamps. Experimentally, he turned the handle again. No good. The clamps stayed fast. Yet there was nothing else that he could turn or pull, and no lock indicating that a key was needed.

'I'm tired of this place!' Samuel shouted. 'We've wasted so much time down here, when we should be looking for Erin! Who knows what she's going through right now?' Tending to his toes, he took off his shoe and threw it hard at the door. It landed on the handle, which was resting horizontally, and the weight of it made the handle gently turn clockwise.

To their surprise, the remaining clamps sprang open. Putting his shoe back on, Samuel tugged on the handle, but the door refused to open. 'Oh, for Phlamel's sake, what *now*?'

But this time Johnathan had an idea, and from the Bandits' own hideout, no less. He pushed down hard on the handle. It sank into a groove on the door. Then he released the pressure; the door sprang open. 'Well, that wasn't so hard,' he said, flashing a satisfied grin at Samuel. They stepped through and, as an afterthought, in case anyone was to check the area for signs of intruders, Johnathan closed the door behind them.

Impressively, it merged with the wall on the other side so well that they could hardly tell it was there. Whoever had built this place obviously loved the idea of secret passageways.

The chamber they were in was lit by Kerical lights hanging on long chains from above, and it seemed to interconnect with other chambers, similar to a network of caves. Crates filled with nothing but packing straw were stacked here and there, and the floor was littered with chunks of dried clay.

Samuel picked a piece up, but dropped it quickly, flinching. It was shaped like a human hand, carefully crafted so that details such as fingernails, skin creases, and even the cuticles were visible. 'Did you see that?' he asked Johnathan breathlessly, who was kneeling to examine the other pieces of clay.

'Yes, it's just like these,' Johnathan replied, holding up a clay foot. It, too, was incredibly detailed. And there were more of them: legs, arms, collarbones, an ear, and part of a face, including a nose and one eye. The eye was the only part that didn't match the rest, for neither the iris or pupil had been shaped. It was just a smooth oval, blankly staring up from beneath long lashed lids.

Carefully finding as many matching pieces as he could, Johnathan began placing them together, trying to make a whole. When he was finished, he stood back, taking a sharp breath. Even though some parts were missing, he could see that the pieces had formed a sculpture of a naked woman, not posed like an art piece would be, but lifeless, like a corpse.

A hacking cough sounded somewhere from another chamber, echoing through to where they stood. Instantly alert, they extinguished the lantern and sunk into the shadows from the Kerical lights. They waited, hardly daring to breathe, but saw no one.

The cough came again, more violently this time. Whoever was making it sounded seriously ill.

Moving silently, they crept forwards in the direction it emanated from, staying close to the walls just in case someone came in. They turned a corner ... and saw why the person hadn't moved.

A man, his hair greying and his beard spraying wildly out to the sides, was doubled over a workbench inside a cell, barely conscious. His hands were covered in wet clay where he'd been sculpting the body of a woman almost identical to the broken one they'd found. His ankles were shackled together, and through his worn clothes, little more than rags, they could see he was dangerously thin.

'Sir?' Johnathan tried solemnly. 'Can you hear me, sir? Are you alright?'

For a moment, the man didn't respond, but then

he turned his head and his eyes focused on them. Abruptly he jumped up and looked at them properly, shaking, and with a look of intense fear. 'Forgive me, please, I was only taking a short rest,' he croaked. His lips were so dry that they cracked with every word. 'My hands ... they're so cold. If only I had a little warmth, I could work much faster.'

'It's alright, sir.' Johnathan held up his hands to quiet him. 'I'm not sure who you think we are, but we mean you no harm.' He gave Samuel a nudge; his friend was goggling at the man, unsure what to make of him.

'Oh, uh, yes,' Samuel said quickly. 'We won't hurt you. I, ah – who are you, by the way?'

The man studied them nervously and inched slightly closer. 'My – my name?' He pulled at his beard, leaving traces of clay on the hairs. Swallowing, he said, 'Richard ... Pines.'

The penny dropped hard in Johnathan's mind. 'The Alkemical Sculptor from the research facility?'

Samuel stared at him and then back at the man. 'Are you serious? But he disappeared two months ago. This guy looks like he's been stuck down here for years. Wherever here is.'

'So it's only been two months since they took me?' Richard said. He coughed again, and this time flecks of blood splashed on the floor.

'We've got to get you out of there,' Johnathan said urgently, studying the lock on the cell door. It was just a simple tumbler lock, but without anything to pick it with or the right key, it was useless. He checked the hinges for any loose parts or wear, but they were well oiled, and by the shine to them, quite new.

'It's no use, lad,' Richard wheezed, wiping his

mouth. 'I've tried and tried, but all it did was drain my strength. There's only one way I'm getting out of here, and that's by *her* orders. I know what awaits me after, and it's far worse that being in this dismal cell, working and reworking all day and night.'

'A woman has you trapped down here?' Samuel asked, surprised.

'Indeed,' Richard answered quietly. 'I don't know her name ... or wish to know. The sight – and smell – of her are repulsive enough.'

'Repulsive? How so?' Johnathan asked. 'Is she some kind of Wytch?' He tried not to envision Winkit scolding him if she heard him say that. The idea of magic achieving in a few seconds what he, as an Alkemist, could only dream of still made him prejudiced against them.

Richard smiled, revealing several missing teeth. 'Oh no, she's no Wytch. She's more like a *demon*, with mottled, clammy skin, yellow eyes, and a smell like rotting flesh. She's also got a wound on her cheek shaped like a set of measuring scales. A brand mark, I would say.'

'Measuring scales? Then that must mean—' Johnathan began.

'The Nekromancer!' Samuel jumped in.

'Nekromancer? One of those people rumoured to bring others back from the dead? Wrong again, I'm afraid.' Another cough. More blood on the floor.

Unable to bare it any longer, Johnathan took off his coat and pushed it through the bars of the cell. 'Here, I know it's not much, but you must put it on. You've got to stay warm,' he advised, feeling the cold seep into his own body.

'Thank you, lad, though I think your generosity

might be wasted on me. I don't have much time left in this world and when I go, I want to *stay* gone,' Richard said softly, easing the coat over his shoulders and wrapping the belt around his middle, tying it with a knot.

'But I thought you just said this woman *wasn't* a Nekromancer?' Samuel asked, confused.

'She's not. The things she's capable of are far, far worse, and what she's planning with this,' he jerked his head over to the sculpture, 'would make your blood curdle.'

'Why don't you start from the beginning and tell us everything you know,' Johnathan suggested. 'We might be able to find a way to help you.'

A dull scraping echoed around the chamber, followed by the thud of heavy boots striking stone steps, getting closer with each stride. Richard's face drained of what little colour it had. 'You've got to hide. *Now!*' he whispered urgently, ushering them away.

Johnathan and Samuel didn't argue, sprinting back around the corner, where they spotted another stack of crates. They slipped behind them, angling themselves just enough to give them a partial view of the cell.

A tall figure dressed in black from head to toe approached the cell door. In one hand he (for they thought it unlikely to be a particularly broad shouldered, angular woman) had a tray carrying a steaming bowl of gruel and a glass of murky water; in the other jangled a set of keys. They glinted silver in the light, and though it was hard to tell from the distance, Johnathan thought they resembled what he and Erin had found in the medicine cabinet at Cornell's house.

The man undid the cell door, placed the tray on

the floor without even looking at Richard, closed it again and checked the lock, and then left the way he had come. As he was walking away, Johnathan and Samuel had a good chance to examine his walk.

'Doesn't he seem a bit ... stiff?' Samuel whispered. 'Like he's got false legs or something?'

Johnathan nodded. 'It's not just his legs, though. Look at the way he's carrying himself, and the way his hands are swinging at odds with his stride. Normally, it's natural to move opposite arm to opposite leg, but he's moving his arm on the same side as he's stepping. It's almost as if he doesn't know how to move properly.'

They saw the man's boots disappear back up the steps, which they realised were only a little away from the other cells decorating the chamber. They had been so surprised to see Richard that they hadn't noticed either at first, but now they could see the whole place was one big dungeon.

'Johnathan, where even are we? There's nowhere in the whole of Nodnol that has a place like this underneath it!'

'Actually, there is somewhere I wouldn't be surprised to find one, and we can't be all that far from it.' Samuel looked at him blankly, so he expanded. 'The research facility. The levels there go pretty deep. It's not so much of a stretch to think that there might be a few more added on.'

'You're not making any sense at all,' Samuel said dismissively. 'We ruled out the research facility earlier. Erin said herself that her father wouldn't kidnap his own man.'

'No, Samuel, we didn't rule out the *facility*, we ruled out their *involvement*.' Samuel opened his mouth to speak, but Johnathan held up his hand. 'Put it this way, if you had a nest of rats under your house, how would you know it was there?'

Samuel thought about it. 'You wouldn't, unless you saw or heard them. But I don't see—'

'What I'm trying to say is, what if this place is under the facility and Erin's father and everyone else have no idea it's here? Remember the note Mr Edwards made in his folder about the ink specifically being delivered to the *back* gates of the research facility? Alright, we don't know for certain that the vial of ink he stole from the Inker and the ones being delivered were the same, but we *do* know that Inker is supplying the Nekromancer. If the inks are the same, then why would they be delivered to the facility if the Nekromancer's hideout wasn't somewhere near it?'

He stood up, dragging Samuel with him, and headed back to Richard's cell. The old man was sitting on a raised stone slab, intended to be a bed. He was spooning hot gruel into his mouth, but his hands were shaking so much that most of it was spilling into his beard. 'I'm not telling you anything more,' he said, without looking up. 'What goes on down here is dangerous and sickening, and if I did say anything, you'd wish I hadn't.'

'I won't argue with you. You're too weak for that,' Johnathan said, trying to keep the frustration out of his voice. 'But will you at least tell us if you know of any way out of here?'

'Only the way that they come in, up those steps,' Richard mumbled between mouthfuls. 'When they brought me down here, I caught glimpses of several halls. I know one leads to her, and one here, but the other I don't know. Can you not get back the way you came? It would be far safer, believe me.'

'No, even if we did go back, we can't get to the surface.'

'Then I can only wish you luck and give you one piece of advice. If you see or hear anyone, especially her, you run the other way. If they catch you, you won't ever leave.' He went back to his gruel, ignoring them completely.

Johnathan and Samuel watched him, and then turned away to go up the stairs, thankful that the rest of the cells appeared to be empty.

CHAPTER 15

'They've been gone too long. Far too long,' Chester said, pacing about in the hall. It was midnight, and the children had been asleep for hours. He and Jasmine had been listening for Erin, Samuel and Johnathan all evening, but they hadn't seen or heard anything that hinted at their return. Even Winkit, who had been patrolling along the roof, came back without any news.

'There's nothing we can do about it, Chester. The snow outside is turning to hail; it's pitch-black and Erin took the map with her. We don't even know for sure where they went,' Jasmine said from the living room. To ease her anxiety, she had taken to patching some of the more threadbare blankets and darning the children's socks. 'All we can do is wait, and if they're still not back by morning, then we can go looking for them.'

'But I feel so helpless,' he complained, poking his head around the door.

He looked so uneasy that she felt sorry for him. Out of all of them, he was the one who got worried about things most easily, and the only thing she could do to help him was create a distraction. 'Come and sit down. Your pacing is making the floorboards creak and I know, for a fact, that the sound carries upstairs.'

He sat straight-backed and stiff, nervously glancing around.

Jasmine chewed her lip. 'You know, you've never told me why you get so angry when Samuel teases you about me,' she said, pretending to be focused on her sewing. Out of the corner of her eye, she saw Winkit jump onto the mantelpiece, an amused twitch to her whiskers.

Chester coughed. 'It's only because I think it's impolite to insinuate things about others that aren't true. I want to head them off before they come to anything.'

'So ... you're just being gentlemanly, then?' She glanced sideways at him.

He shifted in his chair. 'Yes,' he said quietly. His knee started jigging rapidly with anticipation. Finally, he stood. 'I can't sit here and do nothing, Jasmine. I've got to go and—'

'Thank you, I'd love a cup of tea,' she said with a smile.

'Actually, I was going to say that I'm going out—'

'Into the hall to stop the floorboards from creaking? How wonderful. I think there's a hammer and a few nails in the closet where we keep our instruments. It would make such a difference, I'm sure the children would appreciate it when they come downstairs in the morning.'

'Well, if you think it's important ... but I was going to do it when we had more time, and it is late. I wouldn't want to wake anyone up.'

'You're right, it is late. Perhaps you should do it tomorrow, after you've had a good night's sleep?'

Chester stared at her. 'You know I couldn't possibly get to sleep until the others are back. What if something's happened? What if they need us?'

At last Jasmine stopped pretending to be absorbed in her work and, throwing off the blanket she'd been mending, stood and faced him. 'Chester, you've been dancing about all night, wondering so many "what ifs" that I feel like stamping the words across your forehead!' She took a breath. 'Listen to me closely: there is nothing we can do right now, other than keep order in this house. And if you don't start calming down, I'll force you to,' she said, looking meaningfully at the packets of Johnathan's Alkemical ingredients still on the table where he and Erin had left them.

'You wouldn't! You don't know the first thing about Alkemical remedies. You might poison me,' Chester accused, his voice sounding decidedly weak.

'I'll take that risk,' she said darkly.

Chester whimpered and ran from the room. She and Winkit heard him tread on the creaking floorboards and head up the stairs. They listened for a moment to make sure that he wasn't coming back down again for any reason. Silence.

Winkit looked at Jasmine. 'I presume we're leaving now?' She arched her back in a stretch.

'Yes.' Jasmine threw on her coat from where it was draped across the back of one of the chairs. 'Are you sure your friends will be up for this in such bad weather?'

'They might not all come, but after they had such an exciting time last week, a few are sure to turn up,' Winkit confirmed. She jumped onto Jasmine's shoulder.

Carefully avoiding stepping on the loose floor-boards and touching anything else that might give them away, the two silently left the house.

~

The door at the top of the stairs led Johnathan and Samuel directly out into a deserted hall and, following it along, they came to a small central space, facing the other two halls as Richard had specified. It was dangerously open, but still there was no one about. Even so, they felt too exposed and darted to the side where there were stacks of cardboard boxes, fully sealed and with delivery addresses printed on them with ink that was still wet.

'These must be full of Super Notes,' Johnathan said, shaking one and feeling the weight inside. He checked the addresses on the top; each stack was going to a different person. Just how many Super Note salesmen were there?

'Johnathan,' Samuel said, tugging at Johnathan's shirt sleeve. 'This one has your address on it.'

Johnathan looked. It *was* his address. But how did they know he'd started selling them? He hadn't told anyone that he'd taken on the ones from Mr Edwards, and he hadn't given out his address either.

The Kerical lights above them flickered and, for a second, went out completely. From the corridor closest to them came an agonized scream, but it was sharply cut off. They exchanged glances. 'We've got to check it out,' Johnathan urged.

'And I thought you told Erin that you would stop *me* from doing anything rash,' Samuel said wryly.

'That was different. We didn't expect people to

be getting hurt – well, not *live* people anyway,' Johnathan replied, creeping along the hall, staying as close to the wall as was humanly possible.

Samuel caught up to him, and together they headed to where the scream had come from. It was a room halfway up, but before they could reach it, another figure dressed in black came out, carrying an armload of Super Notes. The notes were wet, covered in a silver liquid that dripped off them onto the floor. As Johnathan watched the figure turn away and continue into another room, he saw that the floor was covered in silver stains, as if the silver liquid regularly dripped on it.

'What do you think that stuff is?' Samuel whispered. 'Is it anything Alkemical?'

'Nothing that I've ever heard of. Come on, let's get closer.'

They inched further up until they were right at the edge of the doorway. Johnathan's heart was beating savagely, so much that he was concerned it might give them away, but no one else came out into the hall.

Inside the room, they heard someone speaking. It sounded like a woman's voice, but it was slightly slurred. Straining their ears, they listened.

'I don't know why you're all sitting there cowering. This is a far better fate than the one you would have had if I'd left you in prison. Criminals all, only death in a barren cell awaited you. Yet now you have a chance to go beyond death and return as my servants, bodiless yes, but not without power or purpose. Your magic may change somewhat, but you will still have it, and its potential will be even greater than it is now.'

There was a pause, in which they heard someone being dragged across the floor, the creak of a metal hinge, and a gate being firmly shut. 'It will be over quickly as long as you don't resist.'

There was a clicking of a dial being turned. Then the screaming began. Swallowing, Johnathan chanced a glance inside the room, trying to keep as much of his body hidden as possible. What he saw made his hands shake so much that Samuel had to grab them to stop them from banging the wall. He pulled Johnathan back as the screaming stopped. Johnathan's eyes were wild and wet with tears, and putting his hand to his mouth, he fled back down the hall to the stack of boxes and vomited behind them uncontrollably.

'Johnathan?' Samuel said, patting him comfortingly on the back. 'What did you see?'

But Johnathan couldn't speak. The words wouldn't come to him, despite the images imprinted so vividly in his mind.

Samuel glanced around. If the hall they'd just come from was where 'she' was, and the one leading to the dungeon was now directly ahead, then the one that led to the way out had to be the remaining one, over to the right.

Pulling Johnathan up, Samuel carried him over to it, too disturbed by his friend's behaviour to worry about staying quiet. It wasn't a long hall and, after only a minute, they came to another hatch-like door. He turned the handle anti-clockwise and two of the six clamps lifted off. Remembering the last one, he turned the handle clockwise, and two more clamps released. There were still two left, but now he knew how the hatches worked. Confidently, he turned the handle anti-clockwise once more. It worked and the door was ready to be opened. He pushed the handle down hard into the groove as Johnathan had done, and then let go. The door sprang open.

The smell that hit them from the other side was even worse that the one they'd had to put up with in the green district. It was coming from an old sewer, so covered in cobwebs and grime that it was clear it was no longer serviced – except for a pathway leading to a set of polished metal steps, which were firmly bolted to the wall and wide enough to allow three people to walk shoulder to shoulder.

Leading Johnathan by the arm, Samuel went up them, coming out onto a stone platform where they could still see the sewer below. Further along was another set of steps. When they came to the top of those, however, they found that the last step seemed to carry on into the ceiling. Relighting the lantern now that there were no more Kerical lights, Samuel examined the area where the step and ceiling joined. There was a slight gap between them, but not enough to hook his fingers under.

He turned around, scrutinizing the rest of the ceiling while Johnathan sat down with his head in his hands, trembling. Two hinges had been screwed into it about a metre away, parallel to the last step. Experimentally, Samuel pushed against it. The ceiling lifted up: a trap door.

Peering through the thin gap between the trap door and the floor of the room it opened into, Samuel searched for any signs of movement. The gloom bothered his eyes, but slowly he made out the shape of a pair of shoes, and above them, the hem of a white laboratory coat. One of the researchers!

For half a second, Samuel hesitated, but a

whimper from Johnathan convinced him to open the door fully, regardless of who was in the room. As soon as he did, a wave of cool, fresh air wafted towards them.

Feeling it brush against his back, Johnathan jumped up with sudden energy and pushed past Samuel, clambering out into the room, in full view of anyone inside. What Samuel had taken for a researcher was actually an array of spare clothes hanging on a rail with a number of other outfits, each different to the last. He spotted dispensing aprons, chef whites, a guard's uniform, Doktors' coats, undertakers' suits, oil-smudged smocks and clay-caked overalls, among at least fifty others, complete with matching footwear on a stand beneath them. Some even had name badges and collections of keys tucked into top pockets. There must have been a disguise for every occupation in Nodnol.

Shining the lantern's light around, they saw that the room itself was square and about eight meters wide, with the fresh air they'd felt coming from three large diamond-patterned ventilation bricks spread evenly along one side. On the opposite side were four doors, and one adjacent.

The single door appeared to be metal and had a hole midway up, no larger than the smallest of garden peas, while the other doors were solid wood. Johnathan peered at the small hole and nearly choked with joy. It was a looking hole, filled with glass so that the viewer could easily see what was beyond it. And the sight he saw now was overwhelmingly welcome: the back gates of the research facility, and the street beyond. He'd been right! The tunnel from Cornell's house had led them right under the facility itself.

He made to grab the handle and rush outside, but there wasn't one. Panicking, he turned to Samuel, who was investigating the other doors, pulling them open slightly one by one, revealing dark, brick-built corridors leading into complete blackness. Forgetting his worry, Johnathan briefly wondered where they might have led to, but before he could say anything, they heard heavy-gaited footsteps approach the outside of the metal door. Something about the sound told them straight away that whoever they belonged to was certainly no researcher.

They froze as the footsteps stopped, casting furtive glances at each other. As the door opened, they simultaneously made the same decision, and dived into the rail of clothes, hiding themselves as best they could amongst thick coats and jackets, and extinguishing their lantern once more.

Immediately, the ripe scent of bitter Wytch-weed combined with common lavender filled the room and, straining their eyes as much as they could, they saw an awkward, angular figure enter.

Johnathan knew of only one circumstance where someone would use such a strong-smelling concoction, and that was to conceal the rancid tang of decaying meat. Many of the poorer butchers, and a sprinkling of undertakers, used it on a daily basis, but his gut feeling was that this person was neither of those.

They heard the weight of heavy cloth swoosh to the floor, and clumsy hands fumble with the clothes rail only a few feet away from where they were hiding. Then the figure seemed to draw back and walk over to the trap door. Johnathan felt Samuel fidget and instantly knew why. Neither of they had bothered to shut it.

As if hearing their thoughts, the figure paused, but then carried on to the stairs below. There was a creak and the definite click of something being slotted back into place, and then silence.

They waited behind the clothes for as long as they dared, in case the figure came back, but the only noise was the wind picking up beyond the metal door.

Coming out of their hiding place, stiff with cold and cramp, Johnathan could only point to the door. There was just enough moonlight coming in through the gaps in the ventilation bricks for Samuel to see their problem.

'No handle,' he murmured, furrowing his brow. 'Better just check ...' Tentatively, he placed his hand on the cool surface and pushed.

The door was obviously heavy, but Johnathan saw that it inched forwards slightly. He shook himself and added his strength to Samuel's. The door eased open and without pause they slipped through it and into the freezing night air, barely giving the temperature a moment's thought. Sparing a glance back to make sure it shut properly and, seeing that the outside was covered in brick that blended into part of the research facility's outer wall, they ran over to the back gates. As expected, they were locked, but the spacing on the crisscrossed mesh meant that they had a chance of climbing over and jumping to the ground on the other side.

Taking off their shoes and stringing the laces together so that they could hang them around their necks, they clung to the gates and hauled themselves up and over. Samuel landed feet first onto the pavement, bending his knees slightly to absorb the shock, but Johnathan, his every muscle aching from the cold where he was wearing only a shirt, fell headfirst into a pile of snow.

Shivering, he rolled onto his side and eased himself up on wobbly legs, using the gate to steady his balance. Samuel helped him put his shoes on and let him lean on him as they made their way across the city square towards the house.

A cat yowled as they shuffled past, loud in the quiet of the night. Another joined in and, all of a sudden, eight more appeared, yowling at the top of their lungs. It was only then that they saw someone hurtling towards them, long hair billowing in the wind and cheeks tinged with pink from the cold: Jasmine.

When she reached them, she hugged them both so tightly that they couldn't breathe. Winkit was with her and as soon as they parted, the familiar jumped up onto Johnathan's shoulder.

'My gosh, boy, you're freezing. Jasmine, hand him that blanket you've got rolled up under your coat, quickly!'

Jasmine unbuttoned the top of her coat and removed the blanket, flapping it out and wrapping it around Johnathan like a cloak. 'Th ... anks,' he managed through chattering teeth.

Jasmine wiped away a tear that threatened to freeze on her cheek. 'I'm so glad we found you!' She pulled them into a hug again. 'Chester and I were so worried when you didn't come back. Is Erin with you?' She peered over their shoulders as though expecting Erin to appear.

'No. We'd hoped you'd seen her,' Samuel said.

'What do you mean? Don't you know where she is?' Jasmine asked quickly, her face falling. 'Never mind, let's get back to the house so you can thaw out. Then we'll talk. Perhaps she's managed to send Chester word of where she is.'

Somewhat warmer, and with an escort of cats, Johnathan felt greatly relieved to see Jasmine – so much so that he forgot most of his exhaustion. The horror of what he'd seen, however, haunted him deeply.

When they finally arrived back home and Jasmine and Winkit had thanked the familiars profusely for their help, they found Chester waiting for them in the living room.

Dark circles hung under his eyes, and he appeared to have developed a nervous twitch in his hand. He stood up to greet them, getting out more blankets from the cupboards, but the look he gave Jasmine was so cold that Samuel and Johnathan thought they would have preferred another blast of icy wind.

'You tricked me,' he hissed through grated teeth. 'You sent me upstairs when all along you'd planned to go out after them yourself. *How could you?*'

'I did what I had to, Chester. One of us had to stay here with the children, and you were too agitated to have gone out yourself,' Jasmine said firmly. 'You know I'm right, and I only found them because I had the help of the familiars. Winkit summoned them, and together we searched the city.'

'I *hate* to interrupt,' Samuel said, ignoring their severe stares, 'but can we get to the main issue here? Like figuring out where in Nodnol Erin is?'

'Erin?' Chester asked, suddenly realising that she wasn't there. His anger deflated visibly; the colour left his cheeks in mere seconds. 'Has something happened to her? Why didn't she come back with you?'

'If we knew that, Chess, do you think we'd be asking?' Samuel said dryly.

'I ... suppose not.'

Johnathan stepped forwards, drawing the blanket tighter around his quivering shoulders. 'We think – we think she might – have been taken.'

CHAPTER 16

'Winkit?' Jasmine asked. 'I know you and the other familiars have already helped us twice now, but—'

Winkit shook her head. 'It is our pleasure, and what you're investigating is far more important than us warming ours paws by the fire all night. Besides, I had a feeling we'd be needed again soon, so I asked two of my friends to stay behind with me. They're waiting in the kitchen.'

'Really?' Chester asked. 'I didn't see them come in.'

'The thing about being a cat, and a familiar at that, is we have a way of going unseen when we want to,' Winkit informed him, her green eyes glittering.

'Why would they want to go unnoticed in here? We don't mind,' he said.

'They're drinking milk nipped with a spot of that brandy in the cupboard. I noticed you took care to dust the bottle earlier, so I thought it must have some special value to you. I had to pull the cork out with my teeth, I'm afraid, and I wouldn't normally have touched it at all, but they needed it to warm their bones. They're mistress-less like me, and when a familiar isn't around magic very often, it tends to make them less resilient.'

'Oh,' Chester said dully. 'Well, that brandy was my father's, but if they need it, they can have as much as they want.'

Winkit inclined her head. 'I will check to see if they've finished, and then we shall call back the others and begin our search for Erin. We *will* find her, I promise you.' She jumped from the back of the sofa and ran from the room.

Jasmine and Chester turned to Johnathan, noticing that he was behaving differently. The room was quite warm now, but Johnathan still shook as violently as if he were surrounded by ice, and apart from his speculation about Erin, he hadn't spoken a word.

'I'm going to make some tea, but then I want to know *exactly* where you two were tonight and why Johnathan looks like he's seen a ghost,' Jasmine said to him and Samuel.

She left the room, and the boys heard her taking cups from the cupboard and boiling water on the stove; the whistle from the kettle was muted by the howling of the wind outside. When she returned, she passed them all a cup and saucer and poured tea from a spotted teapot. A packet of vanilla cream biscuits was whipped from the confines of her blouse too, and they all sat drinking and eating, so cosy that their tiredness came back in full.

Jasmine refused to let it take over, however. As soon as Johnathan had drained his cup, she sat staring at him until he noticed her. Their eyes met, but he looked away immediately, suddenly intensely interested in the pattern on the rug.

'Fine, then.' She turned to Samuel.

He took a resigned breath. 'Doktor Cornell's house was in the green district like his file said. It was filthy and bare of nearly everything, but we found a key engraved with the set of scales hidden inside the medicine cabinet. Erin has it still, I think. Anyway, there was a garden at the back of the house with a well, and when I was lowered down into it, we discovered that there was a metal hatch at the bottom. Erin waited at the top of the well while Johnathan and I went down to explore what was under it. We found an ... interesting ... room. There were two tables big enough to lay bodies on, piles of animal bones and some nasty-looking medical instruments. But the most important thing was that there was a secret door leading to a tunnel. We tried checking it, but we'd already been gone for ages and it was long, so we went back up the hatch to call for Erin to reel us up.'

He took another biscuit, crunching it half-heartedly, and then continued. 'Erin wasn't there. We waited and kept calling, but we never heard a response. We had no way of getting out of the well ourselves, so we went back and followed the tunnel. It took us right across the city and led into a dungeon. We found Richard Pines down there, the Alkemical Sculptor who disappeared from the research facility.'

'So, Cornell's responsible for his kidnapping after all?' Chester asked, leaning in closer.

'No, it wasn't Cornell,' Samuel replied. 'It was a woman, and Richard's petrified of her. He says she's worse than a Nekromancer, though he wouldn't tell us exactly what she could do—'

Johnathan sprinted from the room and into the bathroom. They heard him being violently sick.

'What's wrong with him?' Jasmine asked, concern in every line of her expression.

'He saw something down there. The woman was in a room talking to people, saying that what she was going to do to them was better than their fate at the prison where she'd taken them from. I didn't see her, I only heard. It sounded like she was locking someone up in a cage, and then there was screaming. But Johnathan peeked into the room. He's been like *that*,' he paused as they heard Johnathan retch again and whimper, 'ever since.'

'Screaming?' Jasmine poured more tea, draining the pot, and bit her lip. 'Well, if he's not ready to talk about it, tell us the rest of what *you* saw. Did Richard Pines recognise this woman? What does she look like?'

'He would only say that she has strange skin and smells like she's rotting. Oh, she has a brand mark on her face too, apparently. The Nekromancer symbol. I can tell you that she slurs when she speaks, though. It sounded weird, kind of like when you accidentally bite your tongue and try to talk without using it much.'

'Hang around my mother when she's been out drinking with her sister and you'll hear her sound like that too. And as you know well enough, sneaking down back alleys full of rubbish bins can make you smell like spoiled meat and fish. As for strange skin, though ... that could be useful if we find out exactly what condition it is that she's suffering from,' she said, twisting a few strands of hair as she thought aloud. 'It sounds like the only truly identifying feature is the brand. Did Pines know if it was self-inflected, or ...?'

'Richard didn't like talking about her. When we

saw him, he thought we had been sent by her to repri-
mand him for taking a break from his sculpting. He's
working on a sculpture of a woman and said that she
has some kind of plans for it when he's finished. He
thinks she's got plans for him too, none of them nice,
but he's convinced he's dying. He sounded quite
hopeful about it, as though whatever she was going to
do would be worse.'

'Crikey, this is grim,' Chester murmured. 'Is there
anything else you remember?'

'Super Notes,' Samuel stated with a nod. 'Boxes
and boxes of them, addressed to all different people,
including Johnathan. And there were men dressed
completely in black; one of them came out of the
room where the woman was, holding wet Super
Notes that dripped silver drops on the floor.'

'This is getting harder and harder to figure out.'
Jasmine put a hand to her forehead. 'Sculptures and
Super Notes, a smelly woman, and no Doktor Cornell, even though you say this tunnel led from his
house.'

'How did you get out? You didn't say,' Chester
pressed Samuel.

'We found a way into an old sewer, with steps
leading to a door. It brought us to a room built into
the outer wall of the research facility. I think there
are other tunnels that connect to it, because there
were four other doors. There were also stacks of
clothes too, but I have no idea what they were for. We
had to hide when someone – or maybe it was
some*thing* – came in from outside and made down
the steps we had come up from. We legged it after
that and climbed over the research facility's back
gates.'

'So that's why you were so close to it when the familiars found you,' Jasmine commented quietly.

The floorboard in the hall creaked, and they turned to see Johnathan standing in the doorway, his complexion the same colour as the milk on the table. But he had stopped shaking.

'Are you recovered enough to tell us what you saw?' she asked softly.

He sat down heavily in one of the armchairs, pulling the blankets back around him like a cocoon. 'I don't think I'll ever be ready.'

'I can give you some of my father's brandy, if that would help?' Chester offered.

Johnathan gave a weary smile. 'No thanks, it might make me worse.' He ran his hands through his tangled black hair. 'What I saw ... it was like a nightmare. There were prisoners ... chained up and gagged, over in one corner. They were so afraid that they were pulling against their shackles with such force that their wrists and ankles bled. There was a domed cage in the middle, roomy enough for just one person, and it was connected to a series of thick wires that ran through the whole room. I saw *her*. She was turning a dial on the control panel of the cage. A prisoner was inside it and Kerical energy was shooting through their body. They screamed, and—' He made a gagging motion, as if he might throw up again.

Jasmine quickly picked up a charred, empty plant pot from by the window and held it out to him, but he waved her away, regaining control of himself with a deep breath.

'I'm ... I'm okay,' he said after a moment. 'I have to tell you this. It's important. When the Kerical energy hit the prisoner's body, they were ... *transformed* ...

into silver goo. Once the transformation was over, *she* collected the goo and poured it over a plain, single notepad. The moment the goo touched it, it turned into a pad of Super Notes.'

Jasmine clasped her hands to her mouth, and Chester and Samuel paled visibly. 'Then ... when we burnt that one ... the apparition *was* a real person.' Her voice shook.

Without realising what he was doing, Chester took her hand and held it tightly. She didn't ask him to let go.

'Yes. They're real humans, put in there by Kerical energy; lots of Kerical energy. But the worst part is ... *she* was dead.'

'What do you mean?' Samuel asked, his eyes wide.

'The reason Richard told us she smelled like she was rotting is because she *is* rotting,' Johnathan explained. 'The flesh on her arms and neck is black and peeling, and she slurs because her mouth and tongue are falling apart. And her eyes. They can move around and look at things, but her pupils don't dilate or constrict like ours do. They can only stare, unfocused, like glass. The only part of her skin that looks normal is the area around the brand on her cheek.'

Jasmine stood up and paced around the room, deep in thought, oblivious to the fact that the others were watching her. 'What does this mean?' she muttered. 'She's dead but still alive somehow. Who is she? Who is—' She stopped in her tracks. 'Oh, no.'

'What is it? What have you figured out?' Chester jumped up to stand beside her.

She met his eyes slowly. 'Remember the files from

the hospital, the notes from the undertakers saying that the bodies always arrived late from the morgue?'

At her words, it suddenly hit them all.

'Aiyanna Dewfallow,' Johnathan voiced the thought. 'Her body was never found.'

'Then Cornell did it? He actually brought her back from the dead?' Samuel asked, stunned.

'It would appear so,' Johnathan replied.

'Then what happened to Cornell himself?'

'I suspect only Aiyanna would know that,' Johnathan said sombrely.

Erin opened her eyes. Facing her was a high ceiling with dark wooden beams going from one side to the other. Orange shapes danced about on it, and a familiar crackling and popping filled the room. She sat up, greeted by stark white bedsheets that were stiff and smelled like honey. Propping herself against the pillow, she saw a vibrant fire burning behind the grate.

The mantelpiece was mahogany, carved with birds and flowers; she remembered caressing them with her hands when she was a child, delighted at the touch of the smooth wood.

Her room at her parents' house – the last place she had expected to have been taken. Despite her misgivings, the warmth from the hearth and the familiar closeness of all the things she had left behind gave her comfort, and as she could see through the gap in her heavy velvet curtains, dawn had not yet broken.

She thought about the night before, when the men had kidnapped her from the well. After they had tied her up and put her in the back of a motor carriage, they'd injected her with something that dulled her senses. She knew they'd been her father's men; no one else would follow her all that way to the green district and then wait until she was on her own to strike. After the trouble at the research facility and the fact that when he and her mother had tried to force her to marry that awful man, she'd run away, she had expected him to take her to the prison instead. He'd boasted about the wing he now owned. So why had he brought her here instead?'

There was a polite knock at the door. 'Come in,' she said, reaching for a blue silk dressing gown to cover up her nightclothes.

A maid come in that she didn't recognise, carrying a tray with a full pot of tea, two breakfast scones, a small plate of butter, a jar of apricot jam, and a plate of scrambled eggs.

'Begging your pardon for the early hour, miss, but I was instructed by Sir Stronghold to bring you this. He says he wants you to recover your strength from the cold last night and wishes to speak with you when you've finished eating. He's waiting in the dining room.'

'Thank you, I'm ravenous,' Erin said, remembering that she hadn't eaten since lunch the day before. Her stomach rumbled and she blushed. The maid pretended not to hear and carried on pouring tea for her. 'Did you say that my father *wished* to speak to me? He didn't say he demands to, or will force me if I refuse?'

The maid looked confused.

'What I mean to say is: does he not seem angry with me?' Erin clarified.

'Angry, miss? Not at all. If anything, I'd say he was concerned,' the maid replied. She hesitated. 'Will that be all, miss?'

'Yes, I think so,' Erin replied, and the maid curtsied and left the room.

If her father wasn't angry with her after everything she'd done, then did he know something that she didn't? Or was he just pretending – some ploy to make her tell him what she and the others had been looking for at the research facility?

Too hungry to worry for the moment, she tucked into her breakfast, nearly crying at how delicious the scones were. She'd forgotten how talented their cook was.

When she was finished, she set her tray aside and got up, going over to her wardrobe. Her dresses were still hanging inside, along with several new ones, obviously put in there to replace the ones she'd taken with her. There was a new pair of winter shoes as well, and an option of winter undergarments.

Even though she wasn't cold, she clothed herself in the warmest items of the lot, remembering the chill of the night only too well. She opened the door, still surprised to find it unlocked (the idea that the maid might have been lying and that her father wanted to keep her trapped in her room *had* crossed her mind), and went along the grand upper hall to the staircase, where she descended to the first floor and made her way across the marbled entrance hall and into the dining room.

As promised, her father was waiting for her, dressed in a maroon smoking jacket and sporting a clay pipe. He was reading the morning's newspaper, which could only have been delivered a half hour before. He lowered it as she walked in, and she was shocked at the dark circles under his eyes and the worry lines on his face.

'Erin, I'm glad that you've seen fit to join me. I think it's time we had a little chat.'

CHAPTER 17

*H*umphrey snorted in his sleep, startling himself awake. The clock on his bedside table read six-thirty, and no light was coming through his window. He rolled over, sinking his head into the pillow, a snore already threatening in his throat.

A sharp rapping came at the door. Bleary-eyed, he tried to ignore it. The rapping came again, louder and more insistent. He groaned; heaving his sizable bulk from the bed and wrapping himself in his dressing gown, he opened the door.

His neighbour, Johnathan, was standing there, his hand poised in a fist as though he had been in midknock, a look of urgency etched onto his face. 'Humphrey!' He pushed Humphrey back into the room so they could shut the door. 'I need your help.'

Humphrey yawned. The boy was far too energetic for this time of the morning and the cogs in Humphrey's brain didn't start to turn until he'd been fuelled by at least two cups of coffee. 'Whoa there, lad,' he said. 'Sit down on the sofa for a moment while I wake myself up a little, and then I'll hear you out.'

Before Johnathan had chance to answer, Humphrey shuffled into the kitchen and put a fresh pot of coffee on. By the time he returned, with two steaming mugs in his hands, Johnathan was sitting with his hands on his knees, dancing his fingers up and down with impatience. His eyes darted from Humphrey's desk, which was littered with Lectric and Alkemical components from a project he had been working on the previous evening, to the technical and scale drawings of various Kerical machines pinned to the walls.

Humphrey placed a mug on the table in front of Johnathan and gulped down a mouthful of his own coffee while choosing to remain standing. 'Right,' he said. 'Sorry for the lack of neighbourly greeting, but I'm still half asleep. What can I do for you?'

'When we first met the other day, you said you were a Kerical engineer; is that right?' Johnathan asked.

'That's right. Got over twenty years' experience, though it's only in the last few that I've been doing freelance work. Why do you ask?' Humphrey took another gulp.

'Because the help I need is Kerical in nature,' Johnathan replied, picking up his own cup and taking a sip. He pulled a face; it was much more bitter than he had anticipated.

'Is something malfunctioning? A light or a heating device? One of those new Kerical stoves that have just been released?' Humphrey asked eagerly, already forgetting his tiredness.

'No, not any of those, and it's not actually malfunctioning ...' Johnathan struggled, trying to explain the cage he'd seen without giving away what it really did. 'It's a metal frame that you can, uh, put things inside, and when you turn the dial, it changes the thing inside into something completely different. What I wondered was, would there be any way to reverse it?'

Humphrey's forehead creased. 'So, we're talking about a permanent change then, not something like what those expensive washing devices in the laundrettes do, where they only change the fabric into something different until the next wash?'

'As far as I know, the object remains in its altered form until it is destroyed.'

Humphrey whistled. 'That's impressive, very impressive. I know companies that have been trying to do that for years, and none of them could achieve a permanent transformation. I have to ask, though: are you *sure* this machine is Kerical and not just something that's been enchanted? It really does sound too amazing to be true.'

'The, er, cage, we'll call it, was attached to a room full of wires. It made the lights flicker when it was turned on. I don't think a Wytch would bother keeping that sort of detail.'

Humphrey thought about it. 'I suppose not, no,' he finally agreed. 'Alright then, supposing it is Kerical, then to theorise if there's a way to reverse these transformations, I need to know what type of Kerical energy is being used to power it.'

'There're different types?' Johnathan asked, surprised.

Humphrey snorted. 'My gosh, lad, I thought you were an Alkemist too! What have they been teaching you?'

'I was studying to be an Alkemical Apothecary,'

Johnathan replied stiffly. 'I make medicine, not circuitry. I've never had to think about how Kerical energy works.'

'Oh. In that case, I'll let you off.' Humphrey stroked his chin pensively. 'Basically, every Kerical item has a different collection of Alkemical compounds mixed in, with Lectric components dependant on what that item is intended to be used for. One of the first questions that we ask when working out those compounds is: will the item be working with organic matter or inorganic? Take one of the Kerical heart helpers that they implant into people with dodgy tickers to help keep their heart rate at a good pace. The Kerical energy in those has to be compatible with living tissue; in other words, *organic matter*. So straight away we can rule out all the Alkemical compounds that don't work with organic matter and focus on the ones that do. So, tell me, with this cage of yours, what sort of items is it transforming?'

Johnathan hesitated. He couldn't come right out and say that it was people being transformed; Humphrey would think he was off his rocker. And there was always the chance that, if Humphrey *did* believe him, he would go to the police and ask them to investigate. Not only would that result in a series of extremely awkward questions, but they would take so long about it that who knows how many people would have been turned into silver goo by then?

'It was organic, I think. Leaves and twigs, mostly,' he replied eventually. 'Fresh ones.'

Humphrey raised an eyebrow. 'That's even more impressive, transforming items with living cells. What did they turn into afterwards? A different leaf shape? Twigs resembling woods from another tree?'

'Er, silver goo, actually,' Johnathan said quietly.

Humphrey stared at him. 'Well, that's ... interesting. What does this silver goo do, exactly? Is it a fertiliser or some kind of exotic elixir?'

'Do you need to know that to work out if it can be changed back?' Johnathan asked irritably.

'No, I was just curious as to what the point of it was. Having the technology to change the form of something is extraordinary, but if it's only being used to make sludge that serves no real purpose, then it seems a bit of a waste to me.'

'Well, I'm, uh, afraid I don't know,' Johnathan evaded.

'Just where is this cage anyway, lad? Even with what you've told me, I still don't have enough information to give a definitive answer. If I could see it, however, I might come up with something more conclusive.'

Johnathan stood up, putting his unfinished cup of coffee back on the table. 'I'm sorry, but I can't take you to it. It's ... not safe.'

'What isn't? The cage? Or where it's being kept? Because if it's the cage, then you can always shut it down if you think it's a hazard.'

'That can be done?' Johnathan asked, hopeful.

'Of course. All you have to do is disconnect the right circuits. Only a trained Kerical engineer should do it, though; otherwise there's a chance of getting seriously injured if the wrong ones are cut.'

'And that's the only way?' Johnathan asked.

Humphrey nodded. 'That's the only way.'

'Then, thank you for helping me out, Humphrey. I really appreciate it,' he said earnestly and turned on his heels, heading for the door.

'Wait a moment, lad. Are you in some kind of trouble? Why did you come to me to ask all of this, instead of the engineers who made this machine? I know we haven't known each other for very long, but you can trust me,' Humphrey said, following him to the door.

'I'll bear that in mind.' Johnathan broke out into wan smile. 'Thanks!'

With that, he was gone. Humphrey scurried over to the window, looking out. In the Kerical lamp light, he saw Johnathan dash from the building and turn around a corner, out of sight.

Despite the boy's assurances, Humphrey had the distinct feeling that he was heading into something very dangerous. Maybe he should follow him just in case, that way if Johnathan needed help, Humphrey would be on hand. There was more than enough snow around to follow his footsteps.

Johnathan arrived at the house, breathless. The sun had finally risen, and the rest of the household was up and bustling. Excited squeals came from the children as they ran downstairs, discovering that he and Samuel had come back in the night. Heated voices came from the kitchen.

'I think we should have pancakes. The children need a treat,' he heard Samuel say earnestly.

'No, *you* want a treat. There's hardly any nutrition in them at all. The children need something healthy – they've got a lot of growing to do. We should give them whole-wheat bread with butter, fruit, and orange juice,' Chester argued. 'If Erin was here, you know she'd say the same.'

'But she's not, and the children know it. If we give them pancakes, they'll be far too happy to even think about why she's not here,' Samuel pointed out.

'I've got an idea,' Jasmine said icily, 'why don't you two blockheads both make breakfast? Then the children can choose whichever they prefer.'

Samuel mumbled something that Johnathan didn't quite catch. It was followed by the sound of breaking china, which resulted in half a teacup rolling out into the hall, coming to a stop by Johnathan's feet. Jasmine appeared to pick it up; by the crimson flush to her cheeks he was quite convinced that she was the one who had thrown it.

'Oh, you're back already,' she said when she saw him. Her voice sounded weary, but the anger faded from her face. 'Before you ask, Winkit hasn't returned yet. She did send another familiar to say she'd update us every few hours, though, so at least we won't be left in the dark while they're looking.'

The two of them went into the living room where most of the children had gathered, waiting expectantly for their breakfast. Wordlessly, Jasmine and Johnathan moved the sofas aside to make room for the collapsible table stored at the back of the room. They pushed it into place and opened it out to its full size. It wasn't very big, but at least they could lay out the plates for everyone.

'So what did Humphrey say, then?' Chester inquired after bringing in large tray of toast, fruit, and jugs full of orange juice. He glanced at Samuel, who had been pulled over to sit on the floor with the children and tell them stories while they ate. Most of them had chosen to eat pancakes and he was looking rather smug about it.

'He says he needs to see it before he can tell us anything. Apparently, Kerical energy is a lot more complicated than it appears,' Johnathan replied.

'But showing him is impossible,' Chester said, neatly cutting a peach into slices and putting them onto his toast.

'I know that. I told him it was too risky; the cage could be dangerous.' Johnathan took a slice of toast for himself. 'He said if that was the case, we could simply turn it off. And by "simple", he means cutting the wires in one of the circuits, taking care not to get Keri-cuted to death. I left after that. He started asking why I'd gone to him rather than the engineers who built it.'

'Did you answer him?' Jasmine asked, taking the leftover pancakes Samuel had made and dabbing them with mustard from a small jar she'd taken from her vest. Chester looked at her in disgust, but she shrugged and said, 'I like savoury pancakes. Do you have a problem with that?'

Chester shook his head, looking away as she began to eat.

Johnathan smiled at them. 'No, I didn't answer,' he said to Jasmine. 'I couldn't think of what to say.'

'I suppose telling him that the cage was built by a Nekromancer and operated by a dead woman would have been a *bit* hard to swallow,' Chester said, making sure that none of the children were paying attention. He could see Samuel acting out a dramatic scene in the story he was telling on the far side of the room and when he finished, they all applauded.

As the sound of their claps died down, they all

heard an unmistakeable yowling at the front door. 'Winkit!' they said together.

Johnathan rushed into the hall to open it and Winkit stepped inside, shaking snow off her paws. 'Winkit! Do you have news of Erin? Where is she?'

'Hold your rat tails, Johnathan,' she said, flicking her tail in annoyance. 'We still have no news of her whereabouts, but we'll keep looking. The reason I came back is because there's something interesting I think you should see.'

'What kind of thing? Where?' Quickly, he put his shoes and coat back on.

'Follow me and you'll find out,' she said mysteriously.

She led him outside and around the house to where the living room window had been boarded up. There, surrounded by familiars all hissing and bristling their tails, was Humphrey, hastily stuffing a black wire into a small satchel.

'Humphrey! What are you doing here?' Johnathan exclaimed.

'We caught him following you. After you'd gone inside, he attached that wire to the window and held the other end to his ear. We think it's some kind of listening device,' Winkit said.

Humphrey stared at her open-mouthed. 'Johnathan ... is that cat *speaking*? And why have the others surrounded me like this?'

'They're familiars,' Johnathan replied nonchalantly. 'And they're surrounding you because they're our friends and you were doing something suspicious. Now, if you don't mind, I'd like you to answer my question.'

'I will,' Humphrey said in a pained voice. 'But

could you ... call them off or something first? I'm terribly allergic to them.' As if to prove his point, he sneezed hard five times in a row.

Johnathan glanced at Winkit, indicating that it was okay. She gave another yowl and the familiars backed off. 'Thank you, everyone, I'll take it from here,' he told them.

They purred and rubbed against his legs, before heading back off into the snow. Winkit followed.

'I think you'd better come inside,' he told Humphrey, who now had the sense to look guilty.

They made their way into the hall. Humphrey looked dubiously at the blackened walls and floor, but Johnathan assured him that it was perfectly safe.

As if they'd known to expect a visitor, the children all swarmed into the hall the moment Johnathan took off his coat. They gawked at Humphrey, taking in his rounded stomach, black moustache and beard. 'Are you Mr Cinterklaas, the Spirit of Winter who brings children presents?' asked the young girl who'd teased Erin about Johnathan.

Humphrey laughed warmly. 'I'm afraid not, young lady. But if you've been good, I'm sure he'll be around in time for the Winter Celebrations.'

Jasmine, Chester and Samuel came out of the living room, where they'd been in deep discussion and hadn't heard Johnathan come back in. 'All right, children, why don't you all go upstairs and work on those mathematics problems that Erin set you from the workbook?'

'Mathematics is boring,' the girl said, and there were cheers of agreement from the other children.

'I find it quite the contrary,' Humphrey declared.

'Mathematics is a vast subject where there are many puzzles to explore. I use it in my work all the time and, when I do, it's like going on an adventure to find a long-lost treasure.'

'Really?' the children cried excitedly.

Humphrey nodded, and they ran upstairs, making the charred bannister shake.

'So, Johnathan,' Chester said after an awkward silence where everyone stared at Humphrey and he pretended to be completely comfortable. 'Aren't you going to introduce us to your friend?'

'Er, yes. This is Humphrey, the Kerical engineer I went to see this morning. Winkit and the familiars caught him lurking underneath the living room window. He hasn't told me why yet.'

'Alright, alright.' Humphrey put down his satchel and held up his hands in a surrendering gesture. 'I was concerned for your safety when you left my apartment this morning. I only followed you because I thought I could be of some help.'

'What about the wire Winkit saw you using? Was that really a listening device?' Johnathan asked.

Humphrey looked uneasy. 'It does have the ability to make sounds louder and thus eavesdropping is a *tad* easier. Not that I condone such a thing on a normal basis, but when I saw this house with no visible way in, I thought I'd try and listen to what was going on inside, to get a better idea of the situation.'

'And just what did you hear with it?' Jasmine asked briskly.

'Nothing much,' he said evasively. 'Just something about who built the cage Johnathan mentioned earlier.'

Chester narrowed his eyes. 'That was me speaking,' he said. 'You heard me mention the Nekromancer, and the dead woman too, *didn't you?*'

'Something like that, yes ...'

'So, what you're saying is that there's a woman who's been brought back from the dead and is parading around underneath the research facility, turning prisoners into silver goo and using it to make these Super Notes?'

'That's about the sum of it, yes,' Johnathan said bluntly. He and the Bandits had spent the rest of the morning, and a good part of the afternoon, explaining what they had discovered over the past few weeks. Humphrey had listened diligently, but they could tell it was hard for him to accept.

'I suppose you realise that this does all sound rather fantastical? I mean, the idea of human experimentation is one thing; many, many people throughout history have attempted something of the sort, but for them to have succeeded in bringing a person back from the *dead*? I can't believe it. I just can't.' Humphrey twiddled one end of his moustache. 'Are you certain that this Aiyanna doesn't simply have some terrible disease?'

'We showed you her death certificate, right there in her medical files!' Jasmine threw up her hands in frustration, accidentally knocking the tin milk jug onto the kitchen floor. They had just finished a sparse lunch of bread and cheese, complete with tea, and a mug of coffee especially for Humphrey. She cursed with an array of colourful and very descriptive language, which shocked them all into silence (though Johnathan thought nothing she did should surprise him anymore). Picking up a cloth, she mopped up the milk and put the jug in the sink.

Humphrey decided to wait until she was finished before replying. 'Then let me ask another question, if I may?'

'You just did,' she pointed out, dropping back into her chair.

Humphrey coughed politely. 'How can you be sure that this woman from beyond the grave is Aiyanna? And don't tell me that her body went missing, nor that her death was linked with this elusive Doktor Cornell fellow, whose house joins up with the tunnel. I recall that well. Neither are definitive proof, in my eyes.'

She opened her mouth to speak, but Johnathan cut her off. 'Humphrey, you're missing the point. The question of whether Aiyanna is or isn't the woman behind all this is irrelevant. Think about what she's doing! She's stripping people of their bodies to become inanimate objects! She's basically a murderer!'

'And she's kidnapped a very ill man and keeping him hostage in her dungeon,' Samuel added.

Johnathan caught his expression, seeing the same concern as he felt himself. Was Richard even alive still?

'Ah, yes, the Alkemical Sculptor. How does he fit into all of this?' Humphrey pondered aloud.

'That's what we haven't figured out yet,' Chester stated. 'He's making a sculpture of a woman, but why Aiyanna wants it, we don't know. Richard said that's he's been working and reworking it, so she must want it to look like someone.'

'The thing about Alkemical clay is that it's far more durable that normal clay. And the very fact that she kidnapped the top Alkemical Sculptor rather than an ordinary artist is what interests me the most, given that she has a machine that can alter the very make-up of something,' Humphrey considered thoughtfully. He turned to Johnathan. 'The Super Notes, you said they had a bad effect on people – all the families you sold them to were diagnosed with Acute Energy Loss afterwards?'

'That's what Erin told me,' Johnathan replied. 'Ten households in all.'

'Hmmm. It does fit with what I've read in the papers recently, though the articles said that the Doktors who made the diagnosis have no idea why it's affecting people who are so young. It also listed fifteen families with it, not ten, and hundreds of individuals too."

'I'm not the only one who sold them; the boxes we found underneath the facility had addresses of many others, all waiting to be shipped out,' Johnathan said.

'Okay, then. I think I might have a theory, but this is by no means definite. Let's start with the assumption that the Super Notes somehow have the power to drain energy. From the moment they're placed in the house, the whole family would be in close proximity to them, and so everyone within that household is affected. That takes me on to my next thought, which is where does that energy go? If the people put into those notes still have an awareness, however vague, then Aiyanna could have influence over them, and so the energy is possibly being collected for her.' Humphrey paused, checking their expressions. 'Are you all following me so far?'

'I think so,' Chester said and the others murmured agreement.

'Good,' Humphrey continued. 'We also know that Richard Pines has made a clay female body, intricately detailed to imitate the aesthetics of a real one. This clay body has an Alkemical make-up which, though the cage has only transformed organic material so far, could also be altered by it. As I explained to Johnathan earlier, most Kerical machines are built for either organic or inorganic material, but there have been a few rare cases by very gifted Kerical engineers where they've been able to make ones that can be used with both. Now, Johnathan,' he said, turning to him, 'what is the one basic thing that all Alkemical processes do?'

Johnathan started, being questioned so directly. 'They take individual ingredients and combine them to make something new.'

'Exactly. And Aiyanna has two main ingredients: the Alkemical sculpture and the energy collected by the Super Notes. If she puts both in the cage, then theoretically the Kerical currents would not only mix them, but fuse them together entirely, and—'

Something clicked in Johnathan's mind. He stood up abruptly. 'Humphrey, that's it! You've put all the pieces of the puzzle together and given us the answer.'

'I have?' Humphrey said, bewildered. 'I was only

going to say that the combination *might* result in an organic body being formed.'

'Yes, and Aiyanna wants it to be her new body. Her old one's rotting away; if she stays in it any longer, she'll die all over again. But if she has another body to enter, she can transfer herself to it by turning into silver goo and being poured onto it.'

'As I said, this is only a theory. It may not even be possible. And I'm still not sure I believe any of it, either,' Humphrey protested.

'It doesn't matter. It's the only theory we've got and if it's true, then we have to stop her,' Johnathan said urgently.

'How? What can you four do if she's got those guards down there?' Humphrey asked pointedly.

'You mean, what can we *five* do? You're coming with us and you're going to shut off that machine.' He ran out of the kitchen and into the hall, pulling open the cupboard where the Bandit's instruments were. He grabbed them and returned to the kitchen. 'Here, we're going to need these,' he said, to a very startled Jasmine, Chester and Samuel.

'But Johnathan, Erin's not here. The instruments only work if we play together. We told you this before.' Jasmine said, running her hand over her viola case nevertheless, as though her fingers were itching to open it and pick the instrument up, wishing to hear it sing again.

'Hers is the bodhran, isn't it?' he asked.

'Yes, but—'

'Then I'll just have to play it. It's been a while, but my mother had one and every so often she would let me use it. I know it won't sound as good, but it'll be better to take them and try it than just waltzing down there while everyone is alert.'

'Wait a second,' Humphrey said, sounding amused. 'You're not telling me that you youngsters are the famous Musical Bandits now, are you?'

'You bet we are ... and if you've heard of us, then you know exactly what we're capable of! We're not so helpless to stop Aiyanna as you think!' Samuel said, unable to keep the pride he felt from leaking into through his voice.

'That's right,' Chester said, puffing up his chest. 'We *are* the Musical Bandits, and we *can* do this.'

~

It was sunset by the time they left the house. Humphrey, against his better judgement, had agreed to go with them, and after extensive planning, they stopped at his apartment to pick up a few of the Kerical tools he would need, as well as an invention he had been working on.

Mrs Higgins came into the hall as they were clambering down the stairs and demanded to know why he and Johnathan hadn't told her they'd had visitors, but Humphrey distracted her by saying he'd just seen a rat dart behind her and into her apartment. She fled as fast as her stiff joints would carry her, fetching a broom and beating every rug and carpet in sight to see where it was hiding. While she was occupied, they slipped from the building and made for the city centre, heading to the back of the research facility.

They waited in a late-evening café across from it, watching everyone leave the premises. By the time the café closed at eight, the back gates of the research facility were clear of staff and the night had set in fully.

Several familiars were roaming around as they crossed the street to get to the gate. Johnathan stopped briefly to greet them, but they still had no news, so he simply told them to pass the group's whereabouts on to Winkit in case she went back to the house and couldn't find them. The familiars meowed and ran off.

Standing in front of the gates, Johnathan and Samuel took off their shoes, preparing to climb over it as they had before. Now that he wasn't in a mode of sheer panic like the last time he had faced them, it suddenly dawned on Johnathan how high the gates were. A queasy sensation hit his stomach and he turned away to see Humphrey staring at the gates with distinct apprehension.

'You don't really expect *me* to climb over, do you?' Humphrey asked. '*You* might be able to spring up there, but I certainly can't.' He looked purposely at his vast stomach.

'Then how do you plan on getting in?' Samuel asked plaintively.

'With these.' Grinning, Humphrey reached into his satchel and removed what looked like a pair of salad tongs with tangles of black wires attached to the handle. They stared at him as though he were crazy. 'Just watch.'

He grasped the giant padlock that sealed the gates with the tongs and pressed a button on the handle by the wires. The padlock began to heat up, the metal glowing orange and then white. After less than a minute, it melted completely and fell with a splat into the snow. Pleased with himself,

Humphrey stepped aside and pushed the gates open.

'Well,' he said when they didn't say anything. 'Aren't you going to congratulate me for using such an ingenious invention?'

'We wouldn't want you to get a swollen head,' Jasmine smirked.

'That's our Jasmine,' Chester murmured to himself.

She heard him. 'What was that, Chester?' She gave him a long, hard look.

'Oh, nothing.' He flushed slightly and pretended to straighten his coat.

Humphrey coughed, putting away his tongs and asked Samuel and Johnathan, 'Right then, where exactly is this secret door?'

The two boys led the others to the back wall of the research facility, treading lightly in case anyone chanced to be lurking around. Johnathan thought it lucky that the guards only watched over the main entrance, as supposedly there were no entryways into the building from this side.

The wall was greyish stone from top to bottom and the ventilation bricks which Johnathan had hoped would help them pinpoint the door again ran across its entire base. He tried to picture what side he had come out on, but the shock of what he'd seen was still making his memory hazy. He looked across to Samuel, who was veering off to the left corner. 'Are you sure it was over there?'

'Yes, I remember seeing the sign on that café we were just in; it's only visible if you stand over here.' He stopped in front of the wall, running his hand over the surface.

'Uh, chaps,' Humphrey said behind them. 'You do realise that's just plain old solid wall?'

Samuel glowered. 'Well of course it *looks* like that. It wouldn't be a secret entrance if it was in full view, would it?'

As he finished speaking, Johnathan saw two of his friend's fingers sink into the stone. He looked at him incredulously. 'How did you ... do that?'

'It's as I thought. There's two small holes here. I think this is how we open it,' Samuel replied, pulling at the door. It didn't budge.

'With just two fingers? That door's heavy; it's not going to move just from that,' Johnathan said. He felt around the stone too. His fingers passed over what felt like small indents. 'There's more. If you use your other hand as well, and I use both of mine, this might just work.'

'Jasmine, Chester, stand back in case one of those things is in there like before,' Samuel cautioned.

'What about me?' Humphrey asked.

'Just ... stand there and look intimidating,' Samuel replied, once again tugging at the door, this time with Johnathan's help.

Slowly, a seam became visible between the wall and the door, and they it eased open.

'It's much ... harder opening it from this side.' Johnathan commented, straining to keep his fingers locked in the holes at just the right angle. 'How do you think that thing opened it by itself?'

'Well, it sounded more solid than us. Maybe it's got unnatural strength, or something,' came Samuel's uncertain answer as the door finally opened wide enough for them to see inside.

Moonlight shone in the room and they waited

with bated breaths in case anyone charged out. But all was silent inside. One by one, they went in. As Samuel and Johnathan walked over to the trap door in the middle of the floor, Jasmine caught sight of the sheer amount of clothes on the rail. She let out a soft whistle. Nearby, Chester and Humphrey tentatively examined the four wooden doors.

Chester opened one carefully and Humphrey took a miniature Kerical lantern from his bag and shone it inside. Just a few feet in were steps leading sharply downwards. 'If these lead into other tunnels beneath this facility ...'

'They could be a secret path to anywhere,' Chester finished for him. 'I wonder if one comes out near the prison, or the hospital,' he mused. 'That might explain how the bodies of Cornell's patients went missing ... or how Aiyanna got all those people down here.'

A cough from Johnathan reminded them of what they'd gone there to do. Gathering round the trap door, they watched him grasp the thick metal ring screwed into it and heave it open. Samuel held it once it was vertical and helped ease it to the ground so that it made as little noise as possible.

'From here onwards, we have to be extra careful. Stay on guard, if they catch us before we've readied our instruments...' Johnathan said, trailing off as he saw his meaning acknowledged in all their faces.

Humphrey took out several more miniature lanterns and handed one to each person before Johnathan and Samuel led the way down the stone steps of the sewer, wrinkling their noses as the stench hit them full on.

The area was quiet. No movement showed in the

shadows, so they continued on, taking the polished metal steps down to the lower level. Here they saw the Kerical lights lining the wall flicker. Samuel and Johnathan glanced at each other; they knew what that meant only too well.

Coming to the metal hatch, Samuel thought back to how it had opened from the inside and turned the handle accordingly so that the clamps would lift free again. Then he pulled on the door and let go, the reverse of the movement he'd used before, and the hatch sprang inwards, allowing them entry.

The hall was still deserted, but they could hear voices ahead; they were coming from the area where all the halls met. Cautiously, the five of them walked closer, keeping tight to the wall so that if anyone happened to look their way, they could turn off their lanterns and stop in the shadows between the Kerical lights, effectively blending in with the wall itself. Well, Johnathan thought, looking nervously at Humphrey's bulk, *most* of them would blend in.

They were close enough to hear the voices clearly now and they could make out two angular black figures and one skinny one, dressed in Johnathan's old coat. Richard Pines.

He was being pulled along by one of the figures, while the other carried a long, thin wooden crate shaped very much like a coffin. Richard was protesting at being dragged and yanked along when he was perfectly capable of walking himself. The guards were either unconvinced or they simply didn't care, because they only grunted in response and continued on their way, walking him up the corridor leading to Aiyanna.

'Should we follow them?' Chester whispered

after they hung back for a few minutes to make sure the coast was clear.

'I think that's our best option. The closer everyone is, the easier they'll fall asleep when we start playing,' Samuel said. 'Besides, the machine is in the same room as Aiyanna. We have to go there anyway.'

Hurrying this time, while staying alert, they entered the space where the halls joined. Briefly, Johnathan noted that the boxes of Super Notes he'd vomited behind had gone.

They turned and went up the other hall. Richard and the guards must have already disappeared into Aiyanna's room, for there was no sign of them ahead. Johnathan turned. 'It's time,' he whispered. 'Get the instruments ready. As soon as we get near the door and confirm that they and Aiyanna are in there, we need to start playing.'

The Bandits complied, taking their instruments out of their cases and readying them for playing. They got close to the doorway. Prepared for what he might see this time, Johnathan looked in.

There she was, at the far end of the room, which was easily as large as a whole level at the research facility, even more hideous than he recalled. She was busy examining the contents of the crate that the guards had brought in along with Richard. As she bent over and her clothing shifted, it released the stench of her decaying flesh, which even from that distance, reached Johnathan's nostrils in a matter of seconds. 'It's perfect,' he heard her slur. 'You've outdone yourself, old man. And a good thing too. If you had disappointed me again, I would have cast your essence out from that body and used it as a vessel for my mutts.' She indicated the guards.

At this, Johnathan took a good look at them. Now he knew why they walked so stiffly. They were dead too, but if he was interpreting her words right, then she had put the essence of another being into them. He thought of their grunted replies to Richard. It would have been as easy to tell him to stop talking, or ignore him, but they hadn't. And what had Aiyanna just referred to them as? Mutts?

A thought came to him, so strong and disturbing that he couldn't shake it. Surely, she wouldn't have put the essence of dogs into human bodies ... would she?

CHAPTER 19

*J*ohnathan signalled to the Bandits; together they raised their instruments. Humphrey put a hand in his jacket pocket and pulled out two globs of moulded wax and stuffed one in each ear, watching with bated breath as Samuel began the music with his silver flute, a spirited melody that immediately got the attention of the guards inside the room. Johnathan pictured them cocking their heads to one side for a second to determine what the sound was, and even though his nerves were so bad that he was trembling, the thought made him smirk.

He heard them snarling through their decomposing mouths and hoped that by the time they got to the door, he, Jasmine and Chester would have joined Samuel to get the instruments' enchantment to work.

The guards' footsteps thudded closer, but more could be heard, too. Johnathan glanced around the hall and from each end six more guards were thundering towards them. As they all caught sight of the trespassers, they snarled savagely, causing the guards still in the room to do the same.

The bodhran, viola and violin jumped into the music, creating a lively reel that made Johnathan's adrenaline surge through his body. His playing was far better than it had been in their short rehearsal back at the house where they'd practiced on Humphrey and the children. A surge of guilt passed through him as he thought about the children being on their own, but he and the Bandits had promised they would be back before the night was out. And they would be. With an extra spurt of gusto from himself and the others so that their music could be heard throughout the entire underground, he saw the guards finally slow and crumple to the floor.

Still playing, the Bandits and Johnathan made their move into the room, with Humphrey not far behind. Johnathan's stomach gave a flutter when they saw how close the guards had been to the doorway. Interestingly, Aiyanna herself hadn't moved far, only to the spot where the shackles and chains still lay, having restrained the prisoners only the night before. It was as though she had been unconcerned by their music, carrying on with what she was doing and, indeed, as she lay limp on the ground, there was a smile on what remained of her lips, shrivelled so much that it was almost a sneer.

Cautiously, he nudged her with his foot. She was as unconscious as her guards. Johnathan called to Humphrey, who was staring at their bodies with revulsion on his face. Humphrey couldn't hear him; the balls of wax that he'd put in his ears blocked all sound, saving him from being thrown unconscious.

With his hands still occupied, beating the rhythm on Erin's bodhran, Johnathan had to stand right in front of him and signal with his head to get

Humphrey to go over to the cage. With a jolt of understanding, Humphrey did so.

His jaw dropped as he examined it, taking in its domed shape and multitude of wires. He saw the dial which was used to activate it, noting that there were three different settings: organic, inorganic, and a combination of both. It was truly an ingenious invention.

The dial was set into a box-shaped control panel. At the front of it was a door which would gain him access to the cage's main circuitry. The wires that needed to be cut to make the cage defunct would be in there. As expected, the door was welded shut, but Humphrey was well prepared. Out of his satchel he produced a screwdriver, but one that had been heavily modified with Kerical components, and a pair of rubber gloves. Putting the gloves on, he held the screwdriver out so that its tip was in line with the weld, and after winding a small cog on its handle, a beam of blue energy surged from it and onto the metal of the control box. He traced the door's outline with it and, when he was done, the whole door fell out onto the floor, exposing the wires behind. Hastily, Humphrey turned the screwdriver off so that it wouldn't damage the cage's circuitry before he'd had chance to examine it.

It certainly was a complicated set up; he saw now how the different options on the dial worked. There were three main wires each connected to a different bottle full of Alkemical ingredients, forming independent circuits. Depending on the option the dial was turned to, the connecting cable would switch to the appropriate circuit and thus the Lectric current would pass through the circuit and convert into a Kerical one. At that moment, the dial had been set to the organic option and so, when the machine was turned on, it would be capable of transforming human bodies into something else like Johnathan had told him it would.

Up until that point, Humphrey had still doubted the Bandits' story. It wasn't that he thought them liars, but it was so complex that he hadn't thought it possible.

He focused back on his work, remembering that the Bandits had to keep playing for as long as it took him to finish disabling it. He could simply cut the cable from the dial, but that would be too easy to fix. He needed to sabotage it outright, so that there wouldn't be any time to find all the components before he alerted the police to what was going on and they came storming down here to arrest Aiyanna.

He checked the circuitry over once more; there was only one option and even though he was loath to do it on such a fine specimen of Kerical genius, he took a hammer from his satchel and raised it to smash the bottles. He glanced back at the Bandits, who were keeping an eye on the guards while Johnathan stood over Richard Pines, making sure that the old man was still breathing.

Wait, Humphrey thought. He scanned the whole room, searching to the far corners. Aiyanna was gone. He stood up, ready to shout to the others, but then he felt the cool metal of a blade being held against his throat, the stench of death radiating intensely from the hand that held it.

'I wouldn't do that, if I were you,' Aiyanna said behind him, removing the wax from his ears with her other hand. Music suddenly washed over him and his eyes began to droop. 'Drop the hammer and step away from the control panel. Try anything and my knife will wish to greet your voice-box.'

Feeling his body going limp, and with no way of shaking her off, Humphrey did as she said. As the hammer clanged onto the floor, the Bandits and Johnathan looked around. Abruptly, they halted their playing, their mouths agape.

'Oh, the surprise on your faces is priceless,' Aiyanna laughed. It was a stomach-churning gurgle that sounded like someone choking on their own blood. 'I suppose you're wondering why your enchanted instruments aren't working on me. Well, that's the thing about being brought back from death. Your body doesn't respond the same way, and the effects of magic are weak and unreliable ... as the Nekromancer found out when I overcame the magical bonds he'd placed on me to prevent me returning to the surface. Sadly, I can't say the same for my mutts, but then their bodies are not their original ones.'

'When you say Nekromancer, you're talking about Cornell, aren't you?' Samuel asked boldly, dropping his flute uselessly to his side.

'Ah, so you know of him? An unusual man, he was one of those rare male Wytches that only appear every few generations. Quite strong, too, so it was much to my delight when I saw the dismay on his face as I resisted his attempts to control me. I remember the look he gave as I trapped him in his own cage and turned him into liquid silver, which I forced his familiar to drink. Sadly, it went mad and drowned itself in the sewers. *Such* a pity.'

'If you had your revenge, then why have you resorted to all of this?' Johnathan questioned, standing protectively in front of Richard, who remained unconscious. Over by the others, he saw the guards beginning to wake up.

'Why ask a question when the answer is so obvious? Besides, I'm sure lumpy here has already figured it out,' she said, holding the knife tighter against Humphrey's throat.

'So this *is* all to get you a new body, then,' Johnathan conceded.

'Very good. You see, when dear Cornell brought me back, he forgot the one very important thing about using the bodies of people who were already dead. Preservation. By the time he succeeded with me, mine had already started to deteriorate. Of course, bringing my essence back to it has halted the decay considerably, but as you can see, my time is almost up. If I do not transfer myself, then I will die a second time, and believe me, it's not something I care to do. I wish to live the life that was unjustly taken from me, and not spend it down here waiting for every part of me to disintegrate.

'Which is why your arrival here is actually quite fortuitous. I was planning to wait until I received the next lot of energy from the Super Notes, but why should I when the five of you have volunteered yourselves so readily? Four of you are young enough for your energy to be as potent as that which I've been receiving from children, and,' she smiled wickedly at Humphrey, 'anything extra is always a bonus. It should be plenty to top up what I've gathered already and fill the requirements of my transition.'

The guards grabbed Chester, Jasmine and Samuel, and dragged them in front of the cage, gripping their arms tightly so it was useless for them to struggle. Aiyanna looked at Johnathan and raised the muscle where her eyebrow should have been. 'Care to join your friends voluntarily, or do I have to have my mutts drag you—'

The walls of the room exploded in an onslaught of fire and hurtling chunks of stone. Johnathan was knocked off his feet by the tremendous shaking of the ground. Realising that Richard Pines was unable to move, he rolled over to him and used his own body as a shield to protect the older man from falling debris. His friends broke free of the guards, diving to the side in time to avoid the mass of ceiling that caved in, flattening the mutts entirely. Aiyanna had thrown Humphrey down in a dash to escape, but through the settling dust obscuring the fresh hole in the wall, a crossbow bolt sank into her side, sending shocks of visible Lectric through her body so that she spasmed to the floor.

Johnathan craned his head up and saw a cloaked figure holding a crossbow step across the rubble and into the room. The hood of the cloak fell back, revealing long auburn hair and green eyes. Erin!

Arthur Stronghold stood beside her, armed with swords, daggers, ball bombs, and a host of other weapons that Johnathan didn't recognise. Behind him, a troop of his men charged into the room, similarly equipped, and checked the area over to make sure that there were no guards lurking about.

Once they were sure the room was secure, they helped the Bandits and Humphrey up to their feet. Erin rushed over to Johnathan, intending to help him up. 'Johnathan, I—' She stopped sharply as she caught sight of his legs. One of them had been crushed under a large chunk of ceiling.

'I'm ... alright,' he gasped. He could just about see his leg, but strangely there was no pain, only a soft numbness creeping through his body. 'Get Richard and the others out first.'

Erin barked to her father's men and instantly two were at her side, ready to pick Richard up and take him to the safety of the outside, where the Bandits and Humphrey were to be evacuated as soon as they confirmed they could walk on their own.

'Aiyanna,' Johnathan said, trying to ease himself up even as Erin held him down.

Her father saw Johnathan's condition and scurried over to help shift the stone that trapped him.

'We've got her, don't worry,' Erin said softly. 'I shot her with a Kerical bolt, she's not going anywhere unless it's with us. Now hold still; otherwise you'll make the bleeding worse.'

'Erin?' he said as his eyes filled with water. 'I'm glad you're safe. We were all so worried when we couldn't find you.'

'So I heard,' Erin smiled. 'Winkit told me as much, and it's thanks to her that I knew where to come. Now try not to talk. We've got to get you to the hospital.'

~

Johnathan woke to the sound of a Kerical monitor measuring the beat of his heart. His body felt stiff and every joint ached as though he'd been beaten for a week.

The hospital room was stark, only fitted with a bedside table, the medical equipment he was hooked up to, and a tall Kerical lamp, switched off to allow his main source of light to come from the sun rising in the sky, visible through the small window to the side of the bed.

In the corner was a visitor's chair and as he looked, the short blonde-haired girl sitting in it glanced up from her book. 'Molly?' he asked in surprise.

'My parents put me in charge of you while your friends talk to the police and Erin's father. Don't worry,' she added at the concern on his face, 'they're all fine. You're the only one who got injured, though that man you saved is in bad shape. Mother and Father say he's dying, but they can ease his pain to make him more comfortable.'

'I ... I see,' Johnathan said, laying his head against the pillows and gazing up at the white ceiling. For a moment, he couldn't speak, his thoughts clogging his mind. 'He's not in a freezing cell anymore. At least we could do that for him. And I'm glad the others are alright.'

'Johnathan,' Molly said quietly. 'Mother and Father wanted you to know ... they did the best they could with your leg ... and they're sorry they couldn't do more.'

Johnathan sat back up. He wriggled his toes under the covers. Only the ones on his left foot moved. He glanced at Molly, but she deliberately looked away. Carefully, he lifted the sheets to examine his legs.

His mouth went dry. His right leg, up to his knee, had been amputated and fitted with a wooden replacement, strapped on with buckles to his thigh. As he stared at it, he heard Molly start crying. 'I'm so sorry, Johnathan,' she sobbed.

His lips trembled, but he forced himself to smile. 'It's okay, Molly. I'm sure I'll get used to it. It just means I'll be a bit more clumsy than usual, that's all. I suppose it's a good excuse to move out of my apartment so that I don't have to suffer Mrs Higgins anymore. I doubt all those stairs will be good for me while I recover.'

'I'm pleased you said that,' Erin said from the doorway, making them both jump.

Molly got up silently, giving Erin a nod, and left the room.

'I've been having a chat with my father, and he's agreed to let you stay at the family house for a while. Of course, I'm sure the weight of that decision is because he feels terrible for your ... injury. The bomb that caused the explosion is one he'd had the researchers working on for years; unfortunately, they hadn't finished the final testing phase and it caused more destruction than he'd planned. Still, if you do come to live with us, you'll also be keeping the orphans company. I'm sure they'd appreciate it.'

'Your father knows about them?' he asked.

'Yes.' Erin strolled over and sat on the end of his bed. 'He knows about everything now, and while he and Mother don't exactly approve, they decided that my actions were somewhat justified. They know full well that had we not taken them in, most of them would have died on the streets. That's not to say they'll let us off lightly for what we did to the facility, though, but I'm sure it can't be as bad as what we've been through already.'

'I don't know about that. If he hadn't come with you to our rescue, I'd still think he was terrifying.

When I remember how he treated us when we were locked up ...'

Erin pulled a face. 'Mother told me the threats he made were all a bluff. Apparently, he'd been searching for Richard Pines' kidnapper and when he paid a call to Mr Murston to arrange a meeting, he found out that an inspection he hadn't authorised was going on and naturally assumed the kidnappers were back to look for something to do with Pines' work. When he found out it was us, he feared that I'd been caught up in something serious. That's why he did the background checks, and when they came back clean, he was so relieved yet frustrated that he decided to scare us. I'm not entirely sure I believe her, given what Father's like, but she said she told him off something awful for it when she found out. She did agree with him, however, that we should be followed for our own safety, since none of us had owned up to what we were doing.'

'But what about the insane workers he had locked up? He just left them there, mumbling and banging their heads as if he didn't care,' Johnathan pointed out.

'Like I said, my father's not a nice man. Some of his methods are simply cruel. Those researchers were all pushed beyond their limit trying to keep up with his demands and, rather than let them go, he keeps them until a Doktor has assessed them and declared them mentally unstable, at which point they are transferred to an institution far outside of Nodnol so that none of the facility's secrets can be spilled. But now that this has all come to light, hopefully that will change. I won't run away from it this time; I'll stay and demand he puts right every wrong he has ever done.'

'Does he ... does he know anything about how this all started? Why did Cornell *become* the Nekromancer?' Johnathan asked, reaching for the glass of water on his bedside table. It was an inch too far, so Erin got up and handed it to him.

'I don't know. Father hasn't seen fit to discuss any of it with me since the rescue. But I feel like he does know *something*. He's called everyone involved – us, Jasmine, Chester, Samuel, Molly and her parents, Humphrey, Winkit and the young Wytch who stole Mr Murston's keys, as well as Mr Murston himself – to a meeting in a few days. He did ask for Richard Pines, too, but Molly told me he's too weak to be moved. I think he wants to confirm our account of events with his own findings. Hopefully then he'll tell us all the answers to the questions we have.'

'And Aiyanna? Where are they holding her?'

'He should discuss that, too. But for now, you have to focus on recovering. As well as losing your leg, you've bruised your ribs and have severe muscle fatigue. Molly will be back with your medicine soon. Take it and rest.'

hree days later, having been approved by Martha Aqua to get out of bed and try walking around on his new leg, Johnathan was given a message that a motor carriage would be coming to take him to the Stronghold family home.

His body was stiff, and he needed crutches to help him balance, but so far he'd found that his wooden leg wasn't as cumbersome as he'd thought it would be. It was quite light, and the stump it was attached to wasn't sore or aching as the Doktors had warned it might be until it was fully healed.

A Knurse appeared, bringing him his last round of medication before he was sent home, and told him that the motor carriage would be arriving shortly before noon, so if he wished to wash and put on fresh clothes, he had best do it soon.

He thanked her and made his way to the bathroom, resting his crutches against the wall and putting his weight on his real leg so that he could use his arms to wash without falling over. Thanks to his friendship with Molly, the Aquas had allowed him access to private washing facilities normally reserved for patients who were willing to pay an enormous amount of Ren for them. Fresh towels had been laid out for him by the large stone sink, which was pre-filled with warm water, and a variety of soaps were displayed on a stand next to it. He'd thought about having a bath, but he hadn't quite gotten the hang of getting into it by himself using just one leg, so he decided to give it a miss.

Refreshed and smelling like a perfume shop from all the scented soaps, he went back to his room and put on a clean suit that Erin had fetched for him after she'd cleared out his apartment. Even though he was wary of her father, Johnathan had agreed to go and live with the Strongholds until he found another job and could afford a new place of his own. His thoughts drifted to the Super Notes he'd had still boxed up with the rest of his possessions. He wondered if they'd been disposed of, or if the research facility were trying to turn them back into people.

He sighed. At least today he would finally find out.

~

The motor carriage arrived on schedule and Johnathan got in without comment. To his surprise, Winkit was on the back seat, waiting for him.

'It's nice to see you walking about now,' she said, casting an eye at his wooden leg. Even though his trousers hid it, there was still an odd outline from the straps bulging at the joint.

'Thanks,' he said, stroking her behind the ears. She purred. 'Why are you here? I thought you'd already be at the house.'

'Erin sent me. I'm here to keep an eye on your driver.'

'My driver? I didn't catch a good look at him. Is he ... *dangerous?*' he asked, lowering his voice despite the panel between the front and back seats, preventing the driver from listening.

'Not exactly, no. But he's the man who Erin was supposed to marry and he's none too happy with you. Something about a prized set of Angelic Resin. He only agreed to drive you because Arthur Stronghold bullied him into it, though that was because he turned up demanding to speak to Erin and Arthur was short-staffed.'

'Angelic Resin? I don't think I – wait a second.' He stared incredulously at the panel blocking his view to the driver's seat. A memory stirred – him visiting a top Alkemical Apothecary, asking to complete his apprenticeship there and getting so angry with the owner's haughty tone that he'd broken a display. 'You're not really telling me that Alexander Benthas was Erin's unwanted fiancée?'

'The very same,' Winkit said, cleaning her whiskers with one paw.

'I can certainly understand why she ran away then. But why would her parents want her to marry him?'

'Apparently, Benthas Senior and Arthur Strong-hold were childhood friends, and years later, during a drunken night out together celebrating Benthas' discovery of the effects of Golden Shellhorn, which previously had been unknown, Benthas challenged Arthur to a bet that if Erin's mother gave birth to a girl, his daughter would have to marry Benthas' son when they were both of age. Arthur laughed it off, sure that his wife was carrying a boy, but as it turned out, he had to honour that bet,' Winkit explained.

'Erin's future was dictated by a bet? That's outrageous!'

'And Arthur knew it, but still he wouldn't go back on his word.'

The motor carriage pulled into the Stronghold's long gravel-filled drive, stopping outside the front door where a butler was already in position to assist them inside. He tried to open the motor carriage's passenger door before Alexander Benthas could get to it, but Alexander pushed him aside and yanked it open himself.

'We've arrived, *sir*,' he sneered and snatched Johnathan's crutches away from him.

Johnathan had to hold onto the motor carriage's framework to pull himself out of the seat. Once he was standing, Winkit sprang out and leapt up onto Alexander's shoulder.

'Remember what I told you,' she hissed. 'If you harm Johnathan, I'll make it so that you spit hairballs for a month. I imagine your clients wouldn't find that particularly attractive.'

Alexander swallowed and reluctantly gave Johnathan back his crutches.

Winkit jumped down. 'Very good,' she said sweetly. 'Now it would be wise to be on your way.'

Alexander gave Johnathan a last, scathing look and then turned around and got back into the motor carriage, driving off out of sight.

'Would you really have been able to do that?' Johnathan asked Winkit as the butler showed them into the house. The entrance hall was magnificent; the floor was mottled white marble complete with pillars that stretched up to the ceiling. A grand staircase furnished with a deep emerald carpet greeted them and a tall grandfather clock stood to the side, intricately carved with wildlife and a pendulum engraved with a large gilded 'S'.

'Even though familiars don't have their own magic, when they live with a Wytch for as long as I did, certain things rub off. With me, it came in the form of being able to curse people with hairballs,' Winkit replied.

They were directed into the dining room and informed that a buffet of delicacies had been laid out for lunch. However, as they entered, they found everyone waiting for them. Arthur Stronghold sat at the head of the table and on his right was a lady who, by her similar appearance, could only be Erin's mother. She smiled warmly at Johnathan and gestured for him to sit.

Erin sat on her father's left-hand side, with the rest of the Bandits next to her, as well as Molly and a skinny, slightly awkward looking girl who Johnathan didn't recognise. Opposite them were Molly's parents, Lord and Lady Aqua, who had changed out of their Doktors' uniforms and were wearing smart clothing, Humphrey, and Mr Murston, who kept shaking his head at the skinny girl in disappointment. A grey kitten jumped from her lap and greeted Winkit as though they were old friends. Finally, Johnathan realised who she was: Mr Murston's maid, the Wytch, Frances.

Arthur Stronghold cleared his throat as Johnathan took his place at the table, sitting in the empty chair next to Humphrey. 'Now that we are all here, I ask you to forgive me for keeping you waiting for an explanation of recent events. I have spoken personally to most of you and have taken on board all comments and concerns. Before I begin, however, I must tell you that thanks to the help of Frances, an adequately gifted young Wytch, all the families who were diagnosed with Acute Energy Loss due to Super Note exposure have now fully recovered and are free from the disease completely. As an Alkemist, I admit that I am biased against Wytches—'

Erin coughed loudly, giving him a look of intense dislike. He ignored it and carried on.

'—Yet in this case, I have no choice but to admit that Frances has been invaluable to us, succeeding in healing those that our Doktors and the Board of Alkemists could not, by using her magic to return the energy that Aiyanna Dewfallow stole from them by means of those abominable and highly deceptive notepad contraptions.'

There was a slight pause, in which everyone but Mr Murston applauded Frances. Her cheeks turned beetroot red and she stared down at her plate.

'Now,' Arthur continued, 'as for the matter of Aiyanna Dewfallow herself, our sources have confirmed that she was indeed brought back from death by the late Doktor and, as we have found, self-proclaimed Nekromancer, Ichabod Cornell.'

'What do you mean, *self-proclaimed*? There weren't any signs or banners at his house saying, "I am the great Nekromancer, Ichabod Cornell!" that I can remember,' Samuel said pointedly.

Arthur gave him a withering look. 'The key discovered at his address belonged to a box found hidden at the underground site, which happened to contain a personal account of every experiment Cornell carried out during his lifetime, and his reasons for doing so, which I shall explain momentarily,' he advised coldly. 'As I was saying, Aiyanna Dewfallow proceeded to kill Cornell after he'd resurrected her, and she took up the use of his equipment, one very powerful Kerical machine capable of all sorts of obscenities. The machine has now been dismantled and, though not destroyed for the value of its components in Alkemical research, as Director of the Board of Alkemists, I vow it shall never be used again in its completed form. Unfortunately, that means that the victims she turned into Super Notes can never be returned to their original selves, but from consulting with Humphrey here, as the only Kerical engineer who had ample opportunity to assess its inner workings before it was dismantled, my research team told me that the chance of success in doing so would have been very slim in any case.'

'On that matter, may I ask a question, Director Stronghold?' Humphrey asked, half-raising his hand.

'By all means, sir,' Arthur replied.

Samuel glared at him for the drastic difference in his reaction to someone else interrupting.

'Did your researchers discover how the Super Notes stole the energy? I tried to come up with a sound Alkemical hypothesis, but none fit,' Humphrey said.

'Nor would they, however hard you tried,' Arthur said, with a trace of amusement in his voice. 'The women Aiyanna took from the prison were all Wytches, their ties with their community and their familiars severed for the crimes they carried out. Aiyanna chose them for this very purpose, for though she changed their form, she theorised their magic would still be intact, capable of absorbing energy and sending it to be stored underground where she could collect it. Once their new forms could absorb no more, they would disintegrate and become energy themselves, adding to her stores.'

There was an uncomfortable silence and, despite all the food on the table, no one felt like eating. 'So that's why you really brought me home,' Erin said, glowering at her father. 'You didn't want the authorities to put me in prison in case she took me, too.'

'Erin, be silent!' Arthur demanded, but his wife held up her hand to calm him.

'You can't make her keep it a secret all her life, dear. If she wants everyone to know, let her tell them,' she said, giving Erin an encouraging nod.

'Tell us what?' Winkit jumped onto Johnathan's shoulder so that she could view Erin properly.

'I'm a Wytch, Winkit,' Erin said. 'But I have a rare condition, which means that my magic is very unstable and if I try to use it, it takes its toll on my body and reduces my lifespan. That's why I have no familiar; my parents were advised that if I had one, I would be tempted to use my magic, so it would be best not to.'

'A Teeterer,' Winkit murmured. 'Now that you mention it, my mistress Irene did say that there was a Wytch in Nodnol who was one. Supposedly, it mostly affects Wytches who are the first of their power in that linage. I assume that's what you are?'

'We think so,' Erin replied, looking to her parents. 'But we're not sure.'

'I had ... complications before Erin was born,' her mother said, glancing at her husband's hardened brow. 'I miscarried three times, all with twins. So Erin is technically our seventh child. Whether her siblings would have shown signs, had they survived, we don't know. Even Irene couldn't tell us that.'

'So it *was* Irene who gave you advice,' Winkit said. 'I knew she had dealings with a family in high social standing, but I was away on my own business at the time, so I never knew which it was.'

Erin's mother smiled. 'No other Wytch would help us because of how involved we are in the Alkemy world, but Irene didn't care. She knew we were in need, and she helped us.'

Winkit bowed her head, closing her eyes. 'Irene was always like that,' she said softly. She looked up slowly. 'And I think I understand now. She enchanted the instruments for you to help Erin sleep when the magic in her made her restless. Though I didn't know who they were for, I helped her choose them and decide the enchantment. We settled upon having four instruments instead of just one so that it would be harder for anyone to abuse their power and put her to sleep at any time. All the musicians had to be synchronised for it to work. Interesting that they were found again by Erin herself.'

'And used most irresponsibly,' Arthur said, cutting in sharply. 'As my daughter and my wife have now laid themselves bare to everyone present, may I continue? There is much for me to get through.' He stared around the table, meeting everyone's eyes as if daring them to speak otherwise.

'Sir, please tell us why Cornell found it necessary to bring back my niece. Why her? She was such a sweet, innocent young lady, and he turned her into a monster,' Mr Murston said. His voice was strained, as though he had been wanting to ask the question for a while but held back until the right moment.

'For that, we must look back thirty years, to the explosion that blasted all the houses behind what is now Boysenberry Lane – something which I believe you yourself should explain the cause of, Murston,' Arthur said.

Mr Murston shifted in his chair. 'Very well. I know you've been waiting for years to get me to say it out loud.' He gazed around the room, not focusing on anyone. 'I was twenty-seven when The Board of Alkemists was making preparations to fit the first Kerical heating systems in all the houses in those streets. We'd tested and tested them, and finally decided that they were safe for public use. However, there were a few radicals who thought they were dangerous and tried to stir up trouble. I didn't think much of them, and as the project manager at the time, when they showed up on the day work was to begin, I did nothing to deter them. In fact, I thought if we could show them how safely we were working and all the precautions we'd taken, it might convince them that we weren't doing any harm.

'How wrong I was. They'd tampered with one of the units, with the help of some Wytches who apparently felt threatened by our Alkemical advances. But the modification was set to only be effective after the device had had some use – to make it appear as though the units really were unsafe. They apparently had the "sacrifice the few to save the many" approach. So, completely unaware, we fitted them in and everyone counted it as a success. Then two weeks later, one blew up. The explosion caused a chain reaction, setting off the units in every house. Some of the radicals were arrested afterwards and most of the Wytches were rounded up, but as the evidence was hardly concrete after the explosion, only the Wytches, who confessed after receiving much pressure from their community, were imprisoned.' He put his head in his hands, rubbing his face.

Arthur grunted and took over. 'Very bad press, that. Set us back years. The important part is that Cornell lost his family in that explosion. His yearning to see them again spurred him to turn his attention to the stories he'd heard as a child of rogue Wytches trying to bring back the dead. He also studied Alkemy, specialising in Kerical engineering, and then took to medicine specifically to look for good candidates. Even though he knew by then that it was far too late to bring back his family, the idea of cheating death caught in his mind and turned into an obsession. Aiyanna wasn't the first person he tried to bring back, Murston, but when he found her in the hospital and realised she was your niece, he intentionally let her immune system weaken so she died of disease.'

At this, Mr Murston began sobbing. Frances got up to comfort him, but he pushed her away, so she sat back down and paid him no attention.

'His account says that bringing her back and using his magic to make her "haunt" you would have been his ultimate revenge. Fortunately, you need not fear seeing the sorry state we found her in, as the Kerical bolt Erin so expertly shot at her damaged her decaying body so much that it fell to pieces a few hours later, though not before we extracted as much information as possible from her. So, in short, Murston, your negligence is the cause of this whole sequence of tragic events,' Arthur said rather cheerfully. 'And now, with that all straightened out, I believe lunch is getting cold.'

'Father!' Erin jumped to her feet and banged her fists on the table. 'How can you be so insensitive? This wasn't just one person's fault. Everyone makes poor judgements; how could Mr Murston possibly have predicted this?'

'I didn't say he could, Erin. But that's how it is. Not that it matters, everything has been dealt with efficiently and we can all get on with our lives as before, wouldn't you agree, Murston?'

Mr Murston said nothing.

Erin cursed, then shouted, 'Mother, how can you sit there and listen to this? How can you stand him at all?'

Her mother pressed her hands together. 'Oh, Erin. You must know that for all your father's faults, this situation would never have been resolved without him. I know the sacrifices he's had to make over the years to ensure this city runs smoothly and to protect this family. You may not like his methods and, most of the time, nor do I, but that's the way he gets things done. It always has been.' She touched Arthur's arm fondly; he patted her hand in return.

Erin's face drained of colour. 'No ... no, no, no. Can't you *hear* yourself? You sound like a fool, being led around by the nose.'

'That's enough, Erin. I will not have you speak to your mother that way,' Arthur declared, standing up to face her. Their eyes met, neither of them willing to look away.

'You're nothing but a smug, manipulative monster, Father,' Erin said finally. She turned away and strode from the room.

For a few minutes, there was silence as Arthur Stronghold stared at the space where she'd stood. Then, without a word, he sat down and began filling his plate with piles of food, as if nothing had happened.

In one synchronized movement, the Bandits, Johnathan, Molly, Frances, Winkit and Poppets got up and followed after her. As they passed, the butler gave them a discreet nod in the direction of the conservatory. They found her in the corner near a large window, which had been covered by a layer of ice. She was sitting on a wicker sofa, sobbing into its cushions.

'Erin, we've all got family members who are idiots,' Samuel said comfortingly as the Bandits came to sit by her. 'Look at Chester; he's proof!'

Chester thumped him, making the others laugh, but Erin didn't respond.

'Come on, Erin, cheer up. I know he's said much worse,' Jasmine said. 'Do you remember what he told me when he fired me? It shook my confidence so much that I couldn't stand to look in the mirror for weeks.'

'And I don't know him very well, but he does seem perfectly beastly to me,' Molly added. 'Why, if he were my father, I would refuse to speak to him at all.'

Frances murmured her agreement and quietly asked Poppets to sit on Erin's lap so he could soothe her. As he jumped up, struggling because his legs weren't yet strong enough to reach that height, Winkit joined him.

'My mistress wouldn't want you to cry over something like this when she knew all the struggles you overcame with your magic as a child. It's not an easy thing, having that power and not being able to release it. But you've accepted it and have dealt with it beautifully,' she said, rubbing against Erin's shoulder.

Erin sniffed and finally raised her head. She looked at Johnathan. Though he was yet to utter a word, he had been listening with pride to his friends' efforts to ease her sorrow. Now he limped forwards and put a hand on her shoulder. 'I believed you when you said you could change him. I still believe you, and I will help you do it. We all will. So please don't cry, even if he is a terrible excuse for a human being. We're with you on this, and we'll stand by you always.'

Erin's tears doubled, flowing so freely down her cheeks that Winkit and Poppets had to jump aside before they got wet, but this time she was smiling with them.

'I know,' she said.

Dear reader,

We hope you enjoyed reading *Nekromancer's Cage*. Please take a moment to leave a review, even if it's a short one. Your opinion is important to us.

Discover more books by Kathryn Rossati at https://www.nextchapter.pub/authors/kathryn-wells-fantasy-author

Want to know when one of our books is free or discounted? Join the newsletter at http://eepurl.com/bqqB3H

Best regards,

Kathryn Rossati and the Next Chapter Team

You could also like:
Unofficial Detective by Kathryn Wells

To read the first chapter for free, please head to:
https://www.nextchapter.pub/books/unofficial-
detective-middle-grade-fantasy-adventure-kathryn-
wells

ABOUT THE AUTHOR

Kathryn Rossati is a writer of fantasy, children's fiction, short stories, and poetry.

Her interest in writing developed at a young age when she sought to archive all the adventures that magically formed in her head, a result of being on the autistic spectrum and having an image-heavy thought process.

She currently runs a blog where she posts poetry, short stories, book reviews, and writing advice. Some of her earlier works were published under the pen name Kathryn Wells.

Her favourite authors are Diana Wynne Jones, Suzanne Collins, Jonathan Stroud, Neil Gaiman, Garth Nix, J. K. Rowling, and David Eddings, to name but a few.

For more information and a complete list of her published works, please visit her website:

http://www.kathrynrossati.co.uk

Nekromancer's Cage
ISBN: 978-4-86747-776-2
Mass Market

Published by
Next Chapter
1-60-20 Minami-Otsuka
170-0005 Toshima-Ku, Tokyo
+818035793528

24th May 2021